The
ROSETTA COIN

The
ROSETTA COIN

Dana Lyons

Black Lyon Publishing, LLC

THE ROSETTA COIN
Copyright © 2013 by Dana McEndree

Our books may be ordered through your local
bookstore or by visiting the publisher:

BlackLyonPublishing.com

Black Lyon Publishing, LLC
PO Box 567
Baker City, OR 97814

This is a work of fiction. All of the characters, names,
events, organizations and conversations in this
novel are either the products of the author's vivid
imagination or are used in a fictitious way for the
purposes of this story.

ISBN-10:   1-934912-60-3
ISBN-13:   978-1-934912-60-7
Library of Congress Control Number: 2013951111

Published and printed in
the United States of America

Black Lyon Romantic Adventure

To my hero,
Randy

CHAPTER ONE

Solomon St. Germain walked deep in the bowels of the Paris morgue. Overwhelming sadness filled his heart, while hopeless despair consumed his soul. "After three thousand years of guardianship—"

The world has finally become too small for a secret of this magnitude.

"Monsieur St. Germain, our sincere condolences for your loss," said Chardolet, the morgue attendant.

Solomon nodded in acknowledgment. Deep in his heart he knew Grandpere was dead, that he and his cousin Henri would finally find their dear Grandpere in this awful place. A solitary tear ran down Solomon's face for his Grandpere, for the end of an ancient quest, and for his failure of the family oath. He wiped at his face, fearing more tears would come before this night ended.

The morgue attendant continued on. Like the gate-keeper to hell, he led Solomon and Henri down a long barren hallway, drawing them ever closer to the end of their options.

Solomon saw the door to their destination. In spite of his efforts to the contrary, his breath stalled in his chest, lodged up against an immovable wall of anxiety.

His steps grew heavy, his feet feeling like they would sink right into the cold, concrete floor until he disappeared.

If only such a simple escape was possible.

"Please, no," he whispered as fear tightened its grip on his heart. He stopped and pressed his fingers to his forehead. His stomach churned with anxiety and his nose burned from the smell of alcohol and industrial disinfectant.

Above ground, a storm raged, the temporal fury matching the grief that filled Solomon's heart. While he had searched these last two days for his missing Grandpere, the City of Light experienced an unrelenting abuse of rain, thunder and lightning.

Now, we have come to this stinking place.

He glanced at Henri, whose unwavering support had helped Solomon through many a tight situation. Henri's rigid lips proclaimed his agony.

Solomon dragged his gaze back to the morgue attendant standing before the final door in this interminable hallway. Chardolet fidgeted with obvious unease, inspiring a new worm of despair to rifle through Solomon's insides. When Chardolet spoke, his apologetic tone fanned Solomon's escalating distress.

"The autopsy—you understand it is the law under such circumstances?" Chardolet pleaded.

A bead of sweat ran down Solomon's back. He peered at the attendant without responding, immobilized by a perverse mix of revulsion and fascination. These emotions twirled sickly in his mind with curiosity and suspicion, bringing even more perspiration to soak his shirt. His mouth went dry as his fears exploded to manic proportions. Desperate, he clamped his lips together and looked around—

But there was no place for him to run. Before this one remaining door, a future never believed possible waited. Henri stepped to his side. Solomon took a slow breath to loosen his constricted chest and nodded, ready to enter.

Abruptly, Chardolet stopped them. "There is one more thing, Monsieur." He cleared his throat to speak, even while he refused to look Solomon in the eye. He pulled a small plastic evidence bag from his pocket. Without looking, he thrust the bag at Solomon.

"Because this had no direct bearing on the cause of death, the authorities are not interested in it," he said in a rush. "Also, you will see in the autopsy report … other unique discoveries, Monsieur."

Fearing what revelations this new discovery might bring, Solomon reluctantly took the bag. Already teetering on the brink of collapse, he fingered the bag's mysterious contents without looking. A suspicion he dared not voice rose inside him. His heart suddenly constricted, thudding uncomfortably slow in his chest, as if unsure it would continue beating. He was too afraid to ask Chardolet—

What do you mean … unique discoveries?

With no time to consider the man's cryptic words, Solomon pocketed the bag. He and Henri shared a glance. Henri shrugged, as baffled as Solomon.

Chardolet opened the door and stepped inside.

Solomon followed cautiously, not ready to make the full commitment. He paused at the threshold, hoping—

Dear God, won't someone say this is all a mistake?

But Chardolet didn't speak. Instead, he strode to the wall of refrigerator drawers. He checked a number and opened a compartment. He pulled back the sheet.

Recognition of Grandpere's pale form brought instant pain in Solomon's throat as a wash of tears poured free, prompting him to gasp for air. His shoulders sagged and his chin dropped. The tears he feared earlier arrived, coursing down his face *en masse*.

He squeezed his eyes tight and covered his face with his hands. Grief and uncertainty whipped through his body. He rocked back, unsteady, battered by a fate he couldn't fathom.

What will I do?

No contingency plan since his family took the ancient oath of guardianship prepared him for this catastrophic moment. He ground his palms into his eyeballs in a futile effort to scrub away the vision of death, to still his rapidly expanding sense of hopelessness.

Henri gripped Solomon's arm, but Solomon knew the duty was his alone. With a ragged breath he swiped at his eyes and pinched the tears from his nose, not caring as he wiped his hands on his trousers.

Finally, Solomon lifted his head and looked at the body lying on the bare steel. He inched closer. His streaming eyes searched the pale features—features he had loved all his life—features now gone hard with death.

"No!" he cried. He grabbed one of Grandpere's rigid hands and bowed his head, sobbing anew until his lungs filled with the foul stink of this unbearable room.

Abruptly, he pulled back and rubbed his blurry vision clear, understanding what had bothered the morgue attendant. He held out what was left of Grandpere's hand for Henri to see.

"Solomon, my God," Henri cried out softly. "What

did they do to him?"

Solomon glanced at Chardolet standing in the hall and out of hearing range. "How …?" Solomon stuttered. He stopped, his throat rigid with fear, an emotion unheard of in the St. Germaine family. "How do I protect the family? How do I keep the secret—from animals that would do this?"

In the cold, dim light of the morgue, Grandpere's pale flesh was savaged. The thumb was lopped off, leaving a vivid stub neatly clipped, smooth and shiny. Beyond the thumb, the first finger was also missing. As was the next. And the next.

Solomon saw not even a pinky remained.

•

Four weeks later
London, England
The St. Germain Townhouse

"Ah, you bastard," Solomon said. "I have you now."

He snatched the page containing the latest scanning report, hope stirring in his heart for the first time in weeks. "I'm coming for you—and you can't stop me," he promised.

He headed for the door, the report in hand. He grabbed his jacket and shouted, "Henri!"

Henri stepped into the hallway with his curious face. "*Oui?*"

"I finally have a hit on that frequency," Solomon declared. "It's in town, out by the river. The GPS is already sent to the limo. Come. Tonight we find the monster responsible for all this death."

They took a private passage from the luxurious townhouse to the basement garage. While Henri checked the area surrounding the Rolls, St. Germain waited behind the closed lift door. This moment of pause always made him uneasy, inciting the hair on the back of his neck to rise with dreadful anticipation. He rubbed at his nape with a nervous hand.

Henri opened the lift door. St. Germain ducked into the Rolls, slipping into the leather seats with fear skittering down his spine. Not until Henri closed the door and fired the engine, did relief settle across Solomon's nerves.

Once on the move, he sank deep into the back seat of the massive limousine. At seventeen-and-a-half feet of reinforced armored steel, the Rolls-Royce had become his refuge these last few weeks. He felt safe and anonymous behind the darkened windows—it was a place he could breathe. If he was a target, as Grandpere had been, then he was a target in motion. He would not let Grandpere's death be in vain.

"No ... not in vain," he whispered, shaking his head. He flexed his fingers and remembered the burning stink of alcohol before tightening his hand into a fist. He let his head fall back with a moan, allowing the pain to wash over him again. These fresh visitations of horror he encouraged, for the anger was necessary to keep his fear at bay.

"Two Keepers of the ancient secret dead," he whispered. "Leaving me the sole custodian."

This was never supposed to happen.

"How can I do this alone?" he moaned.

The enormous scope of his situation dogged Solomon since that rainy night in the morgue. These past four weeks he had searched for the origin of the RFID chip Chardolet handed him in an evidence bag, drawing on all of his considerable St. Germain resources. To-night was his first break.

He pulled down a small worktable and set up his lap-top. The scanning results were from a monitoring sta-tion searching for a specific frequency broadcast. The GPS coordinates were the address for the broadcast of a tracking chip—hopefully one that came from the same source as the one removed from Grandpere. With a little luck, this signal would lead them to Grandpere's murderers.

"Tell me when we are within sight, Henri," he said across the open intercom. He leaned forward and looked out the front window, as though the monster they pursued ran right before the car—so close, and yet just beyond his reach. "Whom else do you target?" he whispered. He sat back, rubbing his temples.

After three thousand years, if the world really is too small, what will I do?

The Rolls came to rest in the shadows, their destina-tion an exclusive home in a neighborhood by the River Thames. The address turned out to be a large brightly lit, eighteenth century estate.

Through the intercom, Henri announced, "We are at Marsten Hall, of Sir Roger Marsten. They are hav-ing some affair this evening. Perhaps we seek one of Sir Roger's guests?"

Absently, St. Germain answered. "Some poor soul. Whoever they are, I pity them. If the signal moves, fol-low, but not too close. I don't want our presence known unless absolutely necessary."

The night sky deepened and St. Germain settled in to wait. "Open the roof, will you?" he asked. The top rolled back, and sultry air thick with the rich scent of honey blossom wafted down around him. The scent inspired a bittersweet smile.

How I despise being this desperate.

Beyond the beckoning lights of Marsten Hall, stars glittered in the darkening sky. They twinkled with promise, inviting Solomon to plead.

"Bring me answers," he whispered. "Please, I need hope."

•

9:30 PM
Marsten Hall

Madelyn Fox stepped through the great doorway of Marsten Hall and paused to eye the butler standing ready to receive her wrap. In spite of the serious nature of her visit, she smiled, remembering how this solemn gentleman helped her learn to tie her shoelaces when she was four years old. As a rambunctious child running though this house, he was her best friend and confidant.

She gave him her shawl and inquired with a whisper, "Well, are they all here this evening?"

Ever proper, he answered smoothly. "It appears so, Miss Madelyn. And they are also on time."

"Don't scold me, Paris. It wasn't easy getting into this dress by myself." She placed one hand on his arm. "I'm here to see Sir Roger about something ... important." She leaned close, her voice deepening, lending a mysterious air to her words. "Something very important." She lifted her brows in a double twitch and winked.

"Ba-ha," Paris burst out. His quick amusement immediately disappeared and he pulled a formal air, replying, "As you wish, madam. And if I might add, Miss Mady, your frock this evening is quite ... fetching." He gave her an eye of approval and finished with a perfect mimic of her double twitching brows.

Mady laughed. "That's good, Paris, because tonight I am here to fetch."

She walked on to the center of the entry hall and picked up a glass of champagne from a passing tray. The Dom Perignon was crisp against her lips as she surveyed the milling crowd with growing excitement.

Royals and celebrities. Very good, Uncle.

She expected as much at a formal soiree hosted by Sir Roger Marsten for the benefit of the British Archaeological Society. "Get on with it, dear girl," she muttered under her breath, mocking her British half. "Stiff upper lip and all that. Do remember why you're here."

The coin.

With it, she thought, *I will turn this sorry world upside-down.*

Her fingers twitched, insane with the desire to bring the coin and her theory into the public domain. She wanted this more than anything else in her life and she would not be denied.

She slipped into the flow of guests, looking for Sir Roger. She cruised, nodding to this lord, smiling at a rock star, raising her glass in recognition of a colleague in anthropology.

She stopped for a fresh glass and checked the crowded room behind her.

Slowly, her right foot began an unhappy tap.

Now is the time, she thought. After four years of independent research and study, she was ready to share her theory concerning the origins of this unique artifact.

Her one piece of evidence—the coin—was compelling, intriguing and mysterious. But most of all ... it was stunningly undeniable.

The artifact and the realm of possibilities it created had consumed her every waking moment. The countless questions, the possibilities, and the inevitable changes inherent to disclosure—all were a part of the endless cycle stirred to life in her mind.

She ran her hand over the snug silk of her gown. She knew she looked her best, and like her coin, she hoped to also be stunningly undeniable. She felt confident her argument was more than sufficient to warrant the full-scale global investigation she proposed, for her hypothesis and presentation were beyond extraordinary, as was her evidence—tangible proof for the existence of an extraterrestrial civilization on earth.

I will lead the archaeological search of the millennia—a Nobel Prize will be the least of it.

The excitement of discovery sent goose bumps flashing down both arms. When she thought about what all this meant, her stomach fluttered, she forgot to breathe, and her heart set a pace her foot couldn't catch. The time was ripe for the world to know. It was all too much excitement for her to contain.

And too much, she knew, for her to do alone.

She put the brakes on her rampant thoughts and took a deep breath. At the very least, from this night on, her life would never be the same.

I just need someone to believe.

She craned her neck, looking for Roger in the shifting crowd. "Come on, Uncle, you're not that pretty ... where are you?" Her right foot jumped to life again, its beat outpacing the flutter in her belly. She had to find Roger for her disclosure.

Unexpectedly, her single-minded focus cracked under the weight of a nagging thought.

Is he the right one to tell?

Mady snorted and gasped, choking on her champagne. Her foot increased its tempo and she lifted her glass to her face. Behind it, she muttered under her breath. "Don't argue with me about this ... now." She continued to sip her champagne and ignored her inner voice, adding a mumbled curse under her breath.

Unfortunately, for the moment, she needed a facility—one with an attendant. While her lovely gown was spectacular, wearing it did present certain challenges. As she recalled from the fitting, her objections had been creatively dismissed. When she protested with, "I don't think I can sit, much less—" Her worries were waved aside. A very dry, "You will manage, won't you darling?" was all the response she got.

Mady grinned. The occasional runway modeling job did come in handy. Last fall she filled in at the last moment for a sunburned model and got an excellent deal on the dress for her timely cooperation.

And they were right. She was willing to tolerate far more than this wardrobe inconvenience in her pursuit to bring a long overdue enlightenment to the human race about its true origins.

"Whether they want it or not," she muttered.

•

Nicholas Alexander Carter scrutinized the milling crowd in the Marsten Hall entry. He stood alone, elegantly clad, imminently respected, and completely desperate.

"Please," he begged, "let me find success tonight."

His hand slipped into his pocket where the special

artifact rested. His fingers caressed the gold, feeling the symbols on its surface. Since the day he first touched the coin, the mystery of those symbols never let him go. They were always with him, either in his hand, or filling his thoughts.

The enigma presented by the artifact was echoed in the acronym "oopart"—an out-of-place artifact. The coin was out of place, all right.

"No, it doesn't fit at all, does it?" he mumbled. The coin completely disturbed the current model proposed by the so-called experts.

"Fools," he spit with derision. They would argue pointlessly that such a thing could not possibly exist. And yet the gold coin did exist, boldly defying any reasonable explanation.

Because the explanation is ... extraordinary.

Carter caressed the coin as he wandered through the gathering, eavesdropping cautiously here and there in hopes of hearing someone mention this strange artifact they had seen or heard of—

Feigning nonchalance, he shrugged, yet his jaws bulged when he ground them together with frustration. Keeping the coin a secret was necessary. He had to be careful. People were dying.

He swallowed convulsively and his fingers fumbled, losing the coin into the depths of his pocket. An all-consuming fear for what he possessed rippled across his shoulders. He needed help ... from someone who knew about the artifact. Someone who knew where it came from, and what danger the artifact brought.

He needed someone who understood—and wasn't afraid.

●

After being helped back into her dress by the maid on duty, Madelyn returned to the social crush. She made another circuit of the crowd, searching for the still elusive Sir Roger with no luck. Annoyed, she returned to the entryway where Paris maintained his stoic position near the great doorway.

"Paris, have you seen Sir Roger? Does he know I'm here?"

"I informed him myself, madam, not fifteen minutes ago. He searched for you until Lady Somerton waved her checkbook, thereby affecting a coup. I'm afraid you'll have to wait until after dinner, for I see the salon is opening."

Mady groaned when she saw the servants throw open the huge double doors to the grand salon. Paris was right; she would have to wait for Sir Roger. She frowned and mumbled a string of ancient epithets in a forgotten language under her breath.

I will not leave without delivering this proposal.

She stayed with Paris, unwilling to face the salon. She rolled her tight shoulders and smoothed her hands over her dress several times, picking at invisible threads. Her foot tapped about blindly, half interested, before finally running out of steam. She sighed, crossed her arms, then sighed again as she glared at the back of the thinning crowd.

She peeked up at Paris. He eyed her aslant.

"Of course I'm stalling," she said, delivering her words with deliberate Yankee lip, knowing he understood her all too well. She turned her back on him and pulled a model's pose, hipbones out, belly concave, her expression indifferent. Acting as though he didn't exist, she commented to him out of the corner of her mouth.

"You know, it's not fair, Paris, that you are as old as Big Ben ... and know everything."

He grunted a small sound of amusement, but otherwise gave her no words. She turned her head to peek at him, a smile bursting forth when she saw how he mimicked her with his shoulders lifted and his own well-practiced and unaffected expression firmly in place.

Still, she had to go through with this, however distasteful. A snort of disgust and a long breath of resignation served to propel her out of her prognostication. She left Paris and trailed the last of the crowd into the rear of the salon.

Seeing all the seats taken, she muttered, "Good luck standing in these shoes."

•

11:00 PM
Marsten Hall

"Damn it," Carter fumed. Walking around listening to the meaningless chitchat of the rich and aimless made him irritable and restless. By now the entire crowd in the salon was knee-deep in praise for whatever pitiful achievements they might muster.

"Achievements, what a load of crap that is," he swore as he kicked at an invisible demon. A shot of fevered air exploded from the corner of his mouth, carrying his derision out into the night. "The bloody fools," he muttered. "The bloody, damn fools."

He walked to the quiet entryway and stood with his hands in his pockets, scowling. Ending another night with his hopes dashed meant the evening was a bitter disappointment. He was reluctant to leave. He lingered, uncertain, until he heard a subtle throat clearing. Behind him, Paris stood by the door, vigilant as always.

"Paris, good evening, sir. I was wondering, is there somewhere quiet I might—"

"Try the last door on the left, Mr. Carter," Paris responded, pointing with a nod. "It is available, and perhaps may suit your needs."

Pausing to give Paris an appreciative look, Carter walked down the hall indicated and opened the door to a smoking room furnished in late Victorian appointments. Rich, dark cherry paneling subtly accented by vivid red and blue carpets whispered a silent welcome.

From the far end of the room a lone table lamp cast a small warm glow. Straight ahead he saw a bank of floor-to-ceiling windows. To the right, a gas fireplace held a dancing flame. Scattered about the room were several groupings of chairs.

Feeling the need for solitude, he moved to a leather chair by the windows. With the curtains pulled back, the dark night cast a clear reflection of the softly lit room. More than he could ask for, it was perfect for his dejected state of mind.

He sank deep into the chair and pulled the coin from his pocket.

•

"Cripes," Mady muttered as another speaker rose.

In the last two hours every male in the place from highest lord to lowest servant had leered at her. Everyone, that is, except Sir Roger. For all of her efforts, the most she got out of him was eye contact and a shrug as he tapped his watch from across the salon.

She squirmed, her feet unhappy in the high-heels. With no end in sight to the boring applause, she fled the room with a shudder, grabbing a glass on the way.

She needed a place where she could think and be alone, someplace where she could gather her thoughts and rehearse her brief presentation.

"What I need," she announced to the empty hallway, "is a place where I can take off these damn shoes."

She turned right and crossed the foyer, raising her glass in a silent salute to Paris, who nodded in return from his post. She took the east wing and, finding her favorite room, slipped in and eased the door shut.

"Ohhh," she whispered, as she stepped out of her shoes. Leaving them by the door, she padded barefoot across the thick carpets. All wound up with excitement, she paced in front of the small fire.

"I will not lose this opportunity," she said, declaring her intent to the gods. Impatient, she whirled around. She would practice her speech in the comfort and quiet of this room. With her words all sorted out in her head, she could deliver her pitch and then get back to her hotel and change into something a little less stunning.

"Uncle Roger, thank you for giving me your time on such a busy evening," she announced to the fireplace. "I know everyone wants to see you, so I will cut straight to the chase. I'm looking for funding for a worldwide project to search for a special artifact, one of which I already possess. An oopart from a Sumerian site, it is a gold coin, covered with what I think are symbols from an extraterrestrial language.

"I believe the coin is irrefutable proof of an advanced alien civilization on earth during the time of man. I have a full program proposal for this project ready to submit to the Society for funding review."

Her last words rang in the air, disappearing into the plush furnishings. The fire hissed, teasing her ears. She stood with her head tilted, evaluating her speech.

Was I too anxious? Do I sound desperate?

She drew a deep breath for another rehearsal when her ears caught a tiny sound. She listened, mystified, until horror slowly constricted her chest.

Someone's here.

The sound was soft and even ... and came from the window chairs. She whirled, whispering, "Noooo."

As a child, she would hide in these very chairs and eavesdrop on Sir Roger and her mother during some of their more heated debates. She squinted in the poor light. Dismay flooded her when she saw a single, man-sized foot on the floor in front of one chair.

She glared at the foot, uncertain how to proceed. Anger at being listened to without permission flushed through her. She approached the chair. In the reflection in the dark windows, she realized her unknown eaves-dropper was also a voyeur.

He could see me—

Glaring at him in the window, and with her anger slowly on the rise, she watched his eyes boldly follow her through the reflection. She closed in on the high back chair and pulled her gaze from the window to look at the physical form being revealed.

The crown of a dark head of hair appeared, followed by broad shoulders covered in a shamefully expensive black jacket. Next, she spied his lean legs casually crossed as he lounged deep in the comfort of the chair.

From the side, she saw one foot bounced merrily.

Oh, she thought. *He has the gall to appear pleased.* Her lips came together in a tight line and she frowned. *Where do I start?* As she came face-to-face with him, his self-satisfied smirk greeted her. It was too much.

Her ire moved into attack mode.

She curled her bare toes in the thick carpet and wished she wore her shoes so she could maim his shins. "Excuse me," she ground out. "But with all due respect—"

He stood up, completely undisturbed by her charge.

She saw the corners of his mouth twitch in amusement. "You ... you dare to mock me?" she stuttered.

"Madam, I protest, for in that gown it is you who dares a great deal." He looked at her with obvious meaning and pursed his lips in a silent whistle of approval.

Mady bristled. She was about to tell him where his compliment could go—when she saw what was in his hand.

Her exhalation came out with a whoosh, and she felt her mouth hang open in what had to be an unattractive mid-syllable moue. But she couldn't get her lips to respond. All she could do was stare. He artfully balanced a gold coin, weaving it back and forth and in and out of his long graceful fingers.

Is it possible?

She was mesmerized, even though her heart pounded with authority. A rush of tumultuous thoughts passed though her mind, leaving her on tilt and bereft of equilibrium. In her suddenly askew world, she struggled for grounding. She focused on the heavy beaded hem of her gown pooled around her feet, caressing her with the silk lining. When her bare toes squeezed the carpet, the soft wool fibers wafted the soles of her feet. A giddy sensation filled her and she took a step back. Fearing she might fall over, her feet arched and curled in an attempt to grip the carpeted floor.

She called her mind back into operation and forced

her chest to ease up so she could speak. "Is it?" she managed in a half-choke. Raising her eyes to his face, she tried to say more, but her vocal chords refused the call to service. Silence throbbed, painful and embarrassing in the wake of her very recent verbal outrage.

"Nicholas Carter at your service, dear lady," he said.

Mady noted the smooth, rich voice and its teasing tone, registered the words, and recognized the name. But she couldn't take her eyes off the coin. It danced and tumbled through his fingers. When it disappeared, her breath hitched. When it reappeared, she squelched a small sigh of relief.

She pulled her eyes off the coin to glimpse his face. He grinned, his eyes taunting and mischievous, even as he bowed with a gentleman's élan. In a smooth flourish, he snatched the coin from its dance and presented it to her.

"Please forgive me for not announcing my presence earlier, but how else, dear lady, would I have the opportunity to ask if your coin looked something ... like this?"

All the air in the room shifted, leaving a vacuum where Mady stood. She tried to speak and croaked. Under his cool penetrating stare, she coughed and swallowed with difficulty before trying again.

"So I ... I was right," she stuttered. "There are others." She was awash in a flood of adrenaline. Her fingers twitched like crazed rabbits, screaming for her to reach out and take the coin, yet her muscles were frozen with shock. She clamped her arms to her side and leaned toward him to stare at the side of the coin she could see.

Hieroglyphs.

No!

She quickly shook her head back and forth even

as the implications of what this meant rolled over her. Seconds passed in the pulsing silence while the blood pounded in her ears.

Finally, she blinked and stumbled back to life. "Is there a second language? The second language ... on mine is ... is ... is cuneiform, of course ... from Sumer."

To her own ears, she sounded like a fool and she grimaced. Pushing off her shocked stupor, she reached for his coin with shaking fingers. "Oh, it is more than I imagined ... when ... where did this come from, what dynasty? Where did you find it, how long have you had it? How did you get it?" she begged all in one long gasp.

A quick glance across the coin showed her the familiar alien writing and the pyramid impression. She turned the coin over to examine the hieroglyphics. She read aloud.

"Find your Power within the Greatest Temple."

She cocked her head, eager to understand. "Do you know what this means, Mr. Carter?" Expecting him to reveal some pearl of knowledge about the coin, she waited.

Instead, his face closed and he leaned down to whisper in her ear. "Are you aware of the dangers presented by this artifact?"

Mady looked around the room, even though she felt sure there were no other eavesdroppers. She knew of the danger, and a glimmer of fear rippled through her thoughts. She also could tell Carter was keeping something from her.

We all have our secrets.

Without another word, he reached out and retrieved the coin from her fingers. Holding it up, he read the message back.

"Find your Power within the Greatest Temple."

His voice was deep and smooth, his message resonating with a cryptic and mysterious meaning. While his words gave her no explanation, when their eyes met, the back of her neck prickled. She chewed on her lip while her frantic mind weighed the value of this new evidence. At the very least, this would delay her presentation to Sir Roger.

Don't be a fool, her intuition screamed. *Take this opportunity.*

If she and Carter had coins to compare, this new information may change her proposal. She thrummed her fingers on her hip. The sudden chance to examine this new artifact with Carter was more than she could pass up. She could make an appointment with Sir Roger later.

She watched Carter flip the coin through his fingers once more before casually slipping it into his pocket. All her previous theories on the coin simultaneously collapsed and expanded with the addition of this Egyptian piece. She stalled in silence, trying to put all the pieces back together when the distant sound of his voice pulled her back to the present.

"Madam, it appears we have much to discuss, but you have me at a disadvantage. Please, feel free to enlighten me further."

Mady realized her rudeness and cringed all the way to her bare toes. Immediately she thrust her hand out. When they touched, his fingers were warm and strong.

"Madelyn Rose Fox, anthropology," she said. "Goddaughter to Sir Roger. My mother was Olivia Fox. You may have heard of her work on languages. She and Sir Roger partnered on many projects over the years. He's like family."

A tingle of excitement ran up Mady's back and skittered across her neck. She knew she must look like a fool, but she couldn't help herself. If she had a tail, it would be wagging. Hanging on to his warm hand, she leaned toward him. "Are you any relation to Howard Carter, as in the tomb of King Tut?"

"Yes, a great-great uncle," he replied. "One of many from my family with their hearts in Egypt."

He smiled and Mady's tingle turned around and raced back down to her feet. "Please forgive my earlier behavior, Mr. Carter." She indicated her snug gown, and added, "I'm afraid all the blood has been squeezed up into my brain—you understand it's quite a wonder I'm not dizzy. This is definitely my pleasure. In fact, if I may presume, is it possible for us to leave Marsten Hall? There is somewhere I'd like to go."

He answered, his voice purring with anticipation. "And where would you like to go, Madelyn?"

She paused for the barest second.

Something about him calls for my trust.

She saw no reason to play coy at this point, having just told him her greatest secret. The fact that he, too, had a coin meant he carried the same burden, connecting them to some degree. She felt the heat he radiated and answered with a direct look, arching her brows. She enjoyed the mischief he inspired. "Why, to my hotel room, Mr. Carter. I have something I believe you'd like to see."

His face burst into a smile as he stepped to her side. Presenting his arm, he deepened his invitation with a whisper that fanned her neck, creating new shivers. "Then perhaps I should call you Mady," he responded.

She laughed out loud and he leaned in, boyish and flirty. She accepted his arm and they moved to the door where he picked up her shoes. "May I?" he asked. He handed them to her and then braced her as she slipped them on. With her stilettos in their proper place, they strolled arm in arm from the smoking room. In silent accord, they headed for the entry hall.

In the foyer they stood with Paris while Carter's car was brought around. Mady fidgeted in the silence. There was so much she wanted to say, she was bursting with questions. Unable to contain herself any longer, she blurted out, "I think—"

"We really should—" he said simultaneously.

They stopped at once and clapped their mouths shut, drawing a curious glance from Paris. When Mady looked his way, he arched one white eyebrow in diplomatic enquiry.

She dodged his obvious question by looking at the great clock in the foyer. "It's late—nearly midnight," she said, avoiding his eye. "Tell Sir Roger I'll ring him this week." She shuffled her feet, clumsy with her inability to explain further to her old friend. Finally, she cleared her throat and added, "When he is more available."

The attendant arrived with Carter's car, a sleek and powerful Jaguar sport model. While Mady admired the vehicle, she considered the difficulty of getting into the low seat with the restrictions of her tight gown. The taxi she arrived in was larger and more accommodating.

Carter opened her door. She hesitated, not seeing a way for her to dip down into the front seat. She opened her mouth to speak when he stepped up and looked at her shoes, then back up to her face.

Mady attempted to decipher what he was about.

The heat in his look was contagious, warming her face all the way to her chest. His expression was giving her several messages, most of which weren't any help with the problem at hand. Finally, she got it. "How do you do that?" she asked.

"I thought you did it," he answered, his smile a match to hers.

She chuckled and grabbed his arm before reaching down to remove her shoes again. Bracing herself against him, she then carefully slid into the low car seat. She got settled, and whispered, "Whew," as goose flesh raced down her arm. She suddenly felt as though she had somehow just narrowly escaped with her life.

Carter gave Paris a gentleman's salute and walked around to the driver's side. The younger man's cool demeanor was reassuring, and Mady relaxed, her goose bumps and fear fading away.

The Jag fired up and the engine purred with power. Like a shot, the car whisked them through the great lion-crested gates of Marsten Hall and into the night.

CHAPTER TWO

Midnight
London

"Another night in this hole—"

Jack Greer pulled a sneer as he unlocked the security door recessed in the building's old brick façade. Like a shadow he slipped inside the dark, claustrophobic room, melting into the stygian blackness before the single overhead light came on.

He had fifteen seconds.

"Yeah, yeah," he muttered as he entered his code on the keypad on the otherwise seamless steel wall. He shoved his keys in his pocket just as the little tray slid out. "Right, now you." He pressed his thumb into the pad.

"And, dummy," he mumbled under his breath, "If you haven't figured out who I am by now—"

"Name," stated the genderless voice.

"Jack Greer, Regional Director, midnight shift." He made a face, sticking his tongue out just as the steel wall disappeared laterally, revealing a steep stairwell.

He stared at the hole that waited for him, and his

feet adamantly refused to move. This process of going down into the basement building always felt like a descent into hell ... or his grave.

Which would it be tonight? he wondered.

The insane thought of turning around and leaving—a feat clearly impossible—always crossed his mind, so much so that he periodically entertained the idea of his escape. Such rebellion, however brief, was ultimately immature and illogical, for this entry only went one way. He could stand here all night, but the doors behind him would never reopen. Going forward was his only option.

"Of course," he mumbled. Bitter regret reminded him his options were already selected. His heart hammered, bringing a bloom of sweat across his palms.

"Too late," he ground out. He closed his eyes and exhaled, blowing the air up into his face in a vain attempt to erase the memories ... and the leer of constantly condemning faces. Hard as he tried, his exhalation was stale and ineffective, erasing nothing. He wiped the sweat gone foul from his hands onto his pants.

His guilt remained, ground into the pores of his life.

Cautiously he descended the dim staircase and stepped before the camera for an eye scan, glaring at it with all the intensity of his considerable animosity. Witless, the camera blinked and the door slid open.

"The library," Greer said. The simple words were more curse than statement.

The facility encompassed one complete city block and was filled with a vast, endless collection of information all taken illegally and without conscience for the private use of The One, known as Maelstrom.

"The One, now that's a face you don't want to run

into on a dark night," Greer snickered, unwilling to utter the name Maelstrom—as if that simple gesture could shield him from Maelstrom's reach. Greer hunched his shoulders against his thoughts as fear bubbled deep in his heart. Back in the day, when his life was worth living, before he discovered there actually was a hell to pay, he had garnered a pretty fierce reputation as an effective, ruthless, cold-blooded operative.

But that was before the dreams—and the faces— came to make his life a constant hell. Now his days tumbled between the lingering hell of his past and the literal hell of his present, leaving him to expect—

"A hell of a future," he stated flatly. He groaned and scrubbed his face. "Well, it's a little late for that," he said sadly. Such wasted thoughts left him uncertain and dry-mouthed. He turned and stalked to his corner office, knowing he had to begin his midnight evaluations.

On his desk he saw a stack of files waiting, and his shoulders drooped. Deep in his neck, a tiny muscle jumped to life and cranked down with a vengeance. As he sank into his chair, his lips curled, and his mouth suddenly felt tacky and dry, as if—

Don't think about it, just don't think—

The phone rang and Greer jumped in his seat. "Damn you." He cursed the phone and clenched his hands, refusing to pick it up, but it kept ringing. "If I could just get out of this office for one stinking night," he whined.

Isn't that where all the troubles started?

"Oh, shut up," he spit, bravely daring the very hounds of hell to get off his back. He scowled and picked up the phone.

•

Midnight
Marsten Hall

In the quiet night outside Marsten Hall, Henri called softly. "St. Germain, we have a vehicle exiting the estate."

St. Germain checked his laptop for movement of the target. "Yes, and so moves our signal. Follow them. Can you see the license plate?"

"*Oui*. It is a Jaguar leaving now and the number is H555C."

St. Germain tapped the information into his laptop. "Follow from a distance. We will have the name soon."

Henri pulled the big car out of the shadows, moving away from the exclusive area on the river. Soon he heard humming coming across the intercom. With great curiosity, he asked, "So, whom do we follow?"

"We follow Nicholas Alexander Carter, a great nephew to the famous archaeologist, Howard Carter," St. Germain said, reading the biography from his laptop. "Mr. Carter is in his thirties and independently wealthy. He is prominent in the field of archaeology, specifically Egyptian antiquities, and it appears his reputation is excellent and authentic. The addition of Mr. Carter to the mix is quite interesting, wouldn't you say, Henri?"

"*Oui*, but there is a passenger, a woman. What about her?"

"We will maintain our distance and see what happens. We'll see what part she plays, if indeed, any at all."

•

Mady stretched her long legs out. The thrum of the Jag's motor vibrated up through the soft leather seat and put a pleasant hum in her lower back. She watched

Carter handle the powerful car, shifting gears and taking the turns with ease.

She relaxed deeper into the seat, setting her tumultuous thoughts free. She had so much she wanted to say, so many questions she needed to ask. With a twitch, one of her bare feet sprang to life, dancing with anxiety.

What should I say? What should I not say?

She recalled the guarded look on his face earlier when she held his coin. What secrets did he keep? She stopped her thoughts and waited for the internal voice to scream panic, but all was quiet—her heart was easy and steady. Where were the inner alarms telling her to hold back? She cocked her head and heard blessed peace for the first time since she decided to tell Sir Roger.

That's a good sign. Just to be sure, she slowed her breathing and counted to twenty, then added five more for good measure, allowing her intuition adequate time to complain.

Still silence. She couldn't ask for more confirmation. She heaved an exhalation of relief and blurted out, "My mother—"

"My Uncle Arthur—"

She looked sharply at Carter and laughed aloud. "We've got to stop doing that; it's getting creepy." She smiled and joked, but it was true they seemed to think along the same path.

"Please, ladies first," he said. "Tell me about your coin."

Mady coughed and cleared her throat. She had never told this story because she was well aware of the dangers involved with her plan to turn the world upside down through disclosure. Such caution had held her silent for years.

Was Carter the right person to talk to?

Should she have waited and talked to Uncle Roger instead? She didn't even know Carter, yet here she was about to show him her coin. She glanced at his hands on the steering wheel. The tanned fingers were clean and strong, their grip on the wheel firm, relaxed. At his neck, the pulse was slow and steady, like hers.

He has a coin. He understands what that means—or at least part of what is involved.

Since her parent's disappearance and her acquisition of the coin, she had become a loner. Through necessity, she developed a keen sense of what people were about. Getting into this car with Carter was not so much a gamble as it was a display of instinct. He was well known within the archaeological community and it was a fluke they had not crossed paths before tonight.

Well, our paths are crossed now.

"I'm hoping you have information that can help me," she said, "because I know so little. Other than the cuneiform message on my coin, all I have is speculation."

She shrugged, openly mystified. "You've already heard my hypothesis about what the coin is and what it represents. In the last four years this artifact has generated endless hours of intense conjecture. Trust me," she said.

"How did you come by your coin?"

She paused, collecting her thoughts. This was the hard part; she hated telling this story. In her lap, her hands came together in the pose for prayer and she smiled. Prayer was something else she done often since acquiring her coin.

"Four years ago my parents disappeared. They left

our home in upstate New York one Friday morning, intending to spend the weekend in the city. They were last seen getting gas at a station near the house, and then they simply disappeared. No trace of them or their car has ever been found."

She stopped to take a breath and look at Carter. His face, schooled into sympathetic understanding, told her one thing. But his hands curled into white-knuckled fists on the steering wheel said something different. Talking quickly, she went on.

"Afterward, when I sorted through their things I found my mother's journal in her private safe, along with the coin. She had discovered it while working on a site in the Tigris-Euphrates valley ... and she suspected its value right away.

"Strange, you know, I recall that summer, Carter. Uncle Roger worked with her on that dig. I was surprised when I read in her notes that she chose not to tell him about it. In spite of their closeness, something about the coin, or him, held her back. In all the years she studied the coin, she was never able to do anything with the symbols beyond conjecture."

She paused, letting the next words squeak through the sudden tightness in her chest. "I can't help but think if I'd gotten my hands on it sooner, if I had deciphered the symbols, they wouldn't have—" She gave up and shrugged, trying to pretend it didn't matter, and knew she failed. Her praying hands had turned into a knot of fingers.

"After four years," she continued, "I can only guess what the symbols are about. Perhaps they are of no real significance after all."

Carter peered at her and she saw his skepticism at

her remark. He turned back to the road, his face as rigid as stone.

Secrets again, she thought. *But does he have answers? What does he know?*

She turned in her seat and grasped his arm. She knew she was talking too fast, but she didn't care. "My hope is to search for more coins, until I find one that unlocks the secret of the symbols. Your coin, which I need to examine further, might hold some of the answers. My theory is that they are leaving us a message."

The night passing by outside the Jaguar caught her eye, and she gazed past him at the blurring lights, hearing exasperation fill her voice. "I just don't know what this message is."

Mady felt her cheeks burn and she snorted with angst. Understanding the symbols and all they represented was her greatest desire—and her greatest fear. The coin and the message she felt the symbols would deliver to humanity had come to mean more to her than anything else in her life. Once she saw the coin with its mysterious unearthly symbols, she was changed.

Excitement for what Carter could bring to this all-consuming mystery fired in her heart. Anticipation took flight in her ankles and her bare feet began stuttering madly in place.

She looked at Carter hoping for more, but his sympathetic eyes revealed little else.

"My mother was terribly afraid," she whispered. "Afraid of what this meant, of what the coin would do. But I'm not afraid." She sighed and released her tangled fingers, then commanded her feet to be still. "I have had this coin and its mystery for four years," she said, feeling the passion clotting her voice. "Or perhaps the more honest assessment is that the coin has had me."

The words now stuck in her throat and she turned back to the window, "I have burned with wanting to know ... with trying to figure out the mystery, to translate their message. To be so close—"

She glanced at Carter. He nodded in understanding, and she felt the tight madness that had bunched in her chest suddenly release. She caught his eye. "The compelling nature of the damn thing is enough to drive one bonkers, isn't it?" She tried to laugh, but her effort withered in a strangled choke.

Seeing they were near her hotel, she continued. "Like my mother, I was hesitant to talk to Sir Roger, in spite of our family ties. In the end, I only went to him out of desperation. He was my single best choice for funding on a project of this magnitude.

"As you heard earlier, I came here with a proposal and a desire to share the story of the artifact. Deep down, I think I needed to just tell someone about it. Knowing how important this was, I couldn't keep it to myself any longer. Now, I'm not alone."

She gazed out the window, a ripple of relief flowing through her for having released the story to another human being after all this time. "Now there is someone else who shares this ... responsibility." She looked back, to catch his eye.

"Someone who understands how it feels to hold the future of humanity in the palm of your hand."

•

12:30 AM
Soho

Mady's hotel was a moderate-priced brick establishment set off from the more crowded avenues. While not luxurious or chic, it was quiet, clean, and near enough to the clubs and eating establishments to be convenient.

They entered the foyer and she went straight to the front desk to ask for her key. The clerk handed her the card. "Is there anything else for you this evening, Miss Fox?"

Mady glanced at Carter. The clerk's question reminded her that this was her last moment to change her mind, to stop this headlong rush into letting someone actually examine her coin for the first time since it came into her life. Her stomach jumped, but her inner voice stayed quiet. She needed to trust Carter.

"Yes, please," she answered the clerk. "I have a package in the hotel safe. May I have it?"

"Certainly, Miss. That should only take a moment."

She waited at the desk, fidgeting, surrounded again by the strain of polite silence. Beside her Carter stood cool and aloof.

The clerk returned, carrying a sealed envelope and a receipt for Mady to sign. With a quick swipe of the pen she gave her signature and grasped the envelope. She hated to let the coin out of her sight or possession. On those rare occasions that she felt compelled to do so, the relief of reclaiming it was exquisite.

She turned to Carter. "I'm on the fifth floor, room 514, near the end of the hall. Normally I would take the stairs," she said, looking down at her high heels. "But perhaps not this time. Shall we?"

The ride in the lift seemed endless. Mady couldn't make small talk with what she had on her mind. She shifted, restless, glancing several times at Carter. His features were guarded again, lost in thought.

At last the doors opened and they proceeded out into the hall. Mady turned toward her room, then stopped mid-stride. She stared down the long stretch of carpeted hall and it spread before her like a gauntlet, yawning in anticipation.

Waiting for her.

She took a step back and shivered. Goose bumps rose up across her arms.

Carter saw her hesitation and her stricken expression. With a questioning glance he reached out and grasped her arms with warm hands. Rubbing briskly, he asked, "Madelyn, what's the matter? Are you all right?"

"No … yes—I mean, it's nothing," she replied with a shake of her head. "Just a cat walked across my grave, I guess. I'm fine, really." She looked up into his searching face and the sincerity she saw strengthened her earlier conviction, helping to dispel her chills. Refusing to give in to a nameless fear, she marched forward with a determined step.

Before they reached her door she glanced at him one more time. When he realized she was watching him, he reached out for her hand, giving it a little squeeze. His touch was warm and dry and his presence reassuring, easing her nerves. He grinned. She smiled tentatively.

She opened the door to her room and her first thought was to extract herself from her gown. She closed the door and turned her back to him. Looking over her shoulder, she said, "Please, will you save me?"

"Certainly," he answered, his voice husky and thick.

Mady felt him touch the dress. In that precipitous moment before the zipper gave way, her senses went on heightened alert. The silence around them shifted, swelling with the pressure of expectation. Somewhere, a clock ticked long seconds from another dimension. All other sound evaporated except for their breathing, but even that stopped.

Anticipation pulsed between them.

Carter held the gown with one hand and gently pulled on the zipper. The slow, seductive hiss of its descent filled the space between them, mesmerizing with escalating intensity. Her gown parted and sudden cool air washed over her back.

"Ohhh," she sighed with a gasp when the confining garment released her.

A sigh of a different nature came from Carter. Mady glimpsed his expression over her shoulder—his face was a vision of sublime appreciation as he stared at her bare backside. She arched her neck, preening as the heat of his gaze landed on her shoulders.

Abruptly, he pulled his hands from her back, breaking the spell. Mady swayed on her feet before snapping back with a start. "Give me a minute, will you," she said. She tossed the envelope on the bed and snatched up a pair of jeans and a light sweater on her way to the bathroom. "I'll be right back."

Carter moved to the window. What Mady glimpsed of his face was brooding. She hurried to the bathroom, leaving the door half opened. In the mirror she watched him gaze out the window, pensive, patient, secretive.

She changed in a hurry and came out wearing snug, low-cut jeans with a zippered front pocket and a soft lilac colored sweater with tiny buttons. She retrieved the envelope from the bed and went to the small table.

Carter joined her, pulling out her chair before seating himself beside her. Outside, he appeared cool and calm, yet the pulse at the base of his throat was strong and rapid.

Mady almost felt sorry for him. *From this moment on, buddy,* she thought, *nothing will ever be the same.* She opened the envelope and extracted a small black velvet bag. Her fingers trembled and he reached out, stopping her.

"We are in this together, Madelyn," he said, his voice thick with emotion. "I know we have just met and are relative strangers, but we share a tremendous bond by our mutual ... possessions. You are displaying a great deal of trust, all things considered, and I am quite aware of your doubts. I have not told you my story yet, but if you'll show me your coin, I'll tell you everything, I promise."

Mady realized he mistook her trembling for doubting him. "It's not that, Carter. I trust you," she said. She shook her head, her brow wrinkled. "You don't—"

—understand!

She didn't bother to finish. He had to see for himself.

The coin tumbled out into her hand. The light caught the rich gold color and came back with small rainbows of refracted light. This time, his eyes were captured by what she held. He took the coin, elation and deep reverence competing in his face. "My God," he stuttered, "it's true."

Mady recognized his expression—it was the same one he wore when gazing at her bare back. A tiny thrill of appreciation for his excitement ignited a fire in her.

He said, "All my speculation, all the endless wild ideas—to see another coin in my very hands ... it's almost too much." He held the coin up to the light and examined the alien script.

When he looked at her sharply, Mady exhaled,

pleased to see the 'eureka' expression exploding across his face.

Now he's getting it.

Carter spoke with a tremor in his voice. "Madelyn, I thought my coin had a pyramid on it because it was found in Egypt. But I see your coin bearing the exact same mark, a steep-sided pyramid design, that, if I am correct, was unknown in Sumer."

She nodded, encouraging him.

"So, Sumer is on the opposite end of the Fertile Crescent—and centuries at the least prior to Egypt and when we believe the Great Pyramid was built, where my coin was found."

With a guarded expression he gazed at her, this time because he realized he approached the fantastic. "The presence of the pyramid links them," he challenged, "and poses the question: what do the two most explosive cultures in human history have in common?"

He looked up, not believing where his own words were taking him. "Are you thinking the race responsible for the alien symbols participated with both civilizations?"

Mady wiggled in her seat, the words ready to burst from her throat. "Until we find something written in the alien symbols, we'll never know for sure. The evidence now is only circumstantial ... but involvement of an advanced civilization would explain many of the questions we have about Sumer and Egypt. Your coin points even more directly to that end."

The gears in Mady's brain were flying as she explained. "The answer, Carter, is in the symbols. Whoever left them went to a lot of trouble to leave us these clues connecting the two cultures. Somewhere, I know there is a message for us to find. The global search I mentioned was to look though the archives around the world for other ooparts like this."

Her fervor was contagious, igniting in Carter's eyes as she rushed on. "That message, Carter, will be the truth," she said. "I will find this message and translate it."

He gazed back with comprehension in his eyes. The pulse at his throat was jumping and his face was flushed. She watched him and nodded with knowing. She was the only person on the planet who could appreciate his discomfort.

"My God," he whispered, grabbing her shoulders. "If you're right, everything will have to be re-written."

"Ah, academia," she said, grinning, "let thy boundaries be heaven-sent."

Carter attempted to wet his lips and failed. Mady went to the small refrigerator for a bottle of water. Coming to his side, she cracked the seal and took a healthy swig before handing him the bottle.

He drank deeply, gulping. When he finally spoke, his voice quivered. "Madelyn, you realize who will want to stop this, don't you?"

"Off the top I'd say most religions and some governments are going to have a pretty tough day when I have my highly publicized disclosure." She winked, adding a casual wave of her hand. "That's their problem, not mine. Can you read the cuneiform?" she whispered. She leaned close, her breath fanning his face.

He shook his head. "No, I'm afraid that my expertise is limited to Egyptian. What does it say?"

Now she was having difficulty speaking. She cleared her throat roughly. "*You are the Children of Gods.*"

"Gods?" Carter asked. He scrunched his nose at the

mystery, laboring to see where this new piece fit in the puzzle. "Now I have to ask you, what does it mean?"

Mady shook her head. "I was hoping you could answer that. Let me see your coin again?"

He sat up with a lurch and the guarded expression came back into his eyes. She let him wrestle with his thoughts, remembering her angst in the Jag before telling him her story. At last he pulled out the coin and handed it to her. She took it, anxious to make sense of the two messages. What did they mean? What are they trying to tell us? She flipped his coin over and studied the hieroglyphs. "Yes, this is just as I thought. *Find your Power in the Greatest Temple.*"

She wanted to make a connection, but nothing called to her. She lifted one hand palm up, mystified and eager for answers. "How is this connected to *You are the Children of Gods*? Because of the exact duplication in the coin design, there is no question in my mind that the two artifacts came from the same source, but what are they trying to tell us?"

She turned the coin over and examined the circle of alien symbols, searching for something new. Going to her work satchel for a magnifying glass, she glanced at Carter. He sat silent with that brooding expression in his eyes, watching her.

Secrets again.

At the table, she adjusted the small lamp to allow more light, then bent close with the glass. Suddenly she drew back and pierced him with a surprised look.

It's all wrong!

Now that she was looking at it with a calm head, she could see the symbols were off. They were close, damn close, but not perfect. She leaned closer and looked again, scanning each impression. They were wrong again and again. She frowned and picked the coin up, hefting it in the palm of her hand. She tossed it, wondering—and froze. She glanced at the coin and then at Carter. Oddly, he was staring at his watch.

What is he up to?

She stood, her lips compressed with merciless intent. Stepping in front of him, her eyes fired, blasting him with a host of silent recrimination. Her heart ran too fast, making her huff and blow, snorting through her nostrils like a winded animal. When she was able to speak, she leaned into his face and slammed the coin down on the table.

"You son of a—"

CHAPTER THREE

Mady's Hotel
Soho

Mady stood with the door to her room opened wide. "Get out, Carter, or I swear, I'll throw you out myself."

Carter cringed at the threat in her words. For the second time in a handful of hours, she was intent on drawing his blood. *This time,* he thought, *she might actually do it.*

Her nostrils flared and her eyes made it clear she was very angry. She was a fire-breathing dragon; facing her was like being within the scorching perimeter of a blast zone.

It was not a good time to want to kiss her.

Seeing he was not about to leave, she abandoned her position at the door, slamming it shut and rattling the doorframe. She began pacing back and forth in the small room, making several circuits while she revved up for her second tirade of the evening. Without the diversion of a gracefully tumbling coin to distract her, she railed on with gusto.

"I don't know what you're up to, but it won't work

with me. What kind of prank is this? And just ... what ... what kind of person are you?" She turned and glared at him, her eyes shining with the glint of promises made ... and promises undelivered. She stabbed him with a gaze that went all the way to his gut.

"I gave you my trust," she fired.

The words were well aimed. She returned to her pacing, waving her arms and moving her hands in strange gestures that Carter thought looked quite threatening.

"First you eavesdrop on me, then you give a speech about trust, now you attempt to pass a fake artifact ... on me?" She stopped with her arms akimbo and asked him point blank. "Do you have a death wish?"

Carter turned his head to hide his grin of approval. She was spectacular. And while her outrage was entirely justified—for he was ashamed for tricking her—he first needed to see her coin, needed to push her to see how she'd react. He regretted deceiving her that way, but he had to test her. And now, he must make her understand the rest. He swallowed his smile and worked up a penitent face.

She made another pass and he stood up, stepping into her path while she made her turn around. Without noticing he had risen, she turned and slammed straight into him. She stiffened, sputtering, rearing back for another attack.

In the pause, he grabbed her by both arms and gave a shake. "You're right," he pleaded. "I'm sorry I deceived you, but I had to be absolutely certain about you ... and your artifact. If you'll hear me out, I can explain."

With a snort of disapproval she shook his hands free and took a defensive stance, staring with eyes still outraged. She drilled him with a look that meant business—and he believed her. "I don't take well to being used and manipulated," she spit. "If you aren't leaving this instant, then you'll do well to remember that in the future."

She backed up a step and crossed her arms. One foot began an explosive tattoo. After a few seconds of thrumming silence, she tersely added. "Go on. I'm listening."

He stepped as close to her as he could without touching her. She reverberated with life and energy, every bit as magnificent in her anger—and passion he suspected—as he imagined. She was pure goddess, a force to be reckoned with, and he pitied anyone who truly earned her enmity.

And yet—

I have to make her understand the danger.

He said, "I have an authentic coin, and like you, it has consumed me since the day it came into my life. I am foolishly driven to keep it with me at all times—yet I'm afraid of losing it, so I had a duplicate made."

He paused, stating pointedly, "I altered it in case something happened and it fell into the wrong hands."

At this, her tapping foot faltered and stopped. Silently, she arched her eyebrows, encouraging him to continue.

"I'm sorry I led you on, but it was imperative I see your coin first," he said. "I had to be sure."

With that declaration, she fired a snort of disgust through her nostrils and the foot started up again.

He reached out and grabbed her. She thrust her chin out, eyes still obstinate and angry, but her mouth had lost its tight line. He stared at her face and admired the delicate texture of her skin. Sadly, they did not have time for what he really wanted to do. He gave an insistent shake until she looked into his eyes. He had to make her see the seriousness of their situation.

"Your mother was right to be afraid," he said. "People are dead because of these artifacts. You admittedly considered some connection existed between the coin and your parents' disappearance."

He let go and leaned back, watching. Waiting.

After a few seconds she nodded, more to herself than him, as though conferring with an inner advisor. She said, "What you say may be so, Carter." She paused to capture his eyes for a direct look. "But you either trust me, or you get out, right now."

He winced, knowing he deserved her chastisement. "Forgive me, please? You're the first person I've shared this with. It's a matter of life and death. You'll understand how protective I am."

She glared at him, not quite mollified. Her eyes simmered, but the foot had stopped. The resulting silence turned stiff as concrete. Neither moved.

Carter coughed.

I have to make her see I'm not the enemy.

He cleared his throat. "If you'll accept my humble invitation, I'd like to take you to my home so you can examine my coin ... the real one."

The fire stirred in her eyes and he dared to hope, for they were going to need each other. "Then I will tell you who has died."

•

On the streets below Mady's fifth floor hotel room, the Rolls-Royce limousine continued to cruise. St. Germain fingered the small plastic evidence bag and recalled the autopsy report. The tracking chip was removed from a knot of old scar tissue.

How did they manage it? When was it implanted?

He gripped the bag in an angry fist. He had to find this predator before the family secret was discovered and taken ... or worse.

Henri spoke, interrupting Solomon's thoughts. "They are on the move again."

St. Germain saw the changing coordinates on his laptop and gave the command. "Maintain our distance."

Sitting back, he returned to his dark speculations while the limousine pursued the unsuspecting pair. Beneath his newfound hope, a silent fear of the unknown remained.

•

1:00 AM
Mayfair

Carter opened the door to his apartment, allowing Mady to precede him into the luxurious two-story home. "Please, make yourself at home," he said. "I'll be right there." He disabled the alarm, taking the time to steady his wild thoughts and heart.

He wanted desperately to regain Mady's trust, but now that he was home, he was nervous and anxious. His heart rattled too fast and his stomach danced around, inspiring sweat to appear in his palms. He rubbed his hands together and turned to watch her, needing the reassurance of her presence.

She wandered through the front room, pausing here and there to admire the art. In one corner she inspected a massive Egyptian funerary collar of lapis and gold. By the time he caught up with her, she was at the goddess collection.

How appropriate, he thought.

He came to her side, close enough to feel her warmth and inhaled lightly, drawing her scent. It was woodsy and spicy, warm and exotic. A shiver shot down his spine and tickled his genitals, then moved out to his limbs. Her independent nature appealed to him and he wanted to know more, much more. Like his father, he was drawn to American women.

Remembering his mother, he spoke, his voice more ragged than he wanted. "CC, Chloe Carter, that's my mother. She was a great believer in the goddess myth; this was her collection. This display is her personal shrine, dedicated to the potential of feminine strength and spirit."

He raised the glass case-cover. In the center of the case two identical statues of gold glowed like warm honey in the light. Beside them, jade and ivory figures bore the classic features of great pendulous breasts and abdomens. Other statues were of delicate alabaster accented in fine detail with copper and gold wire. Tiny one-inch amber miniatures were as smooth as river stones. Others were decorated with mother-of-pearl inlay, garnets and sapphires.

"My mother was a Yank, like you," he said, touching a gold statue with sapphire eyes. Abruptly he lowered the glass cover and turned from the case. "Come on. In here, Mady."

They entered the library. A great bank of windows on the southern side provided an abundant view. The hardwood floors were sprinkled with antique Persian carpets, scattered like jewels. On the walls, book and display cases overflowed with his Egyptian collection. A rare four-foot-tall Egyptian vase dominated one corner, its gold and lapis lazuli accents glittering in the spotlight.

He walked to the bookcases on the east wall and released a hidden catch. The wooden bookcase slid back, exposing a massive wall safe. Mady came to stand behind him.

"I keep my original coin in here under lock and key," he said. "The previous owner of this apartment was a diamond broker with an obsession for safety and privacy. He left behind an impressive state-of-the-art security system."

With a light tap he entered a code and opened the safe door. "I don't think I'm paranoid," he said with a shrug and a wave of his hand. "Just ... appropriately cautious. All things considered, the extra security was a fine selling point when I bought the place."

He glanced over his shoulder at Mady. Her expression was one of fading patience. He knew he was babbling, but he couldn't help himself—he had never shown his coin to anyone before.

"In addition to what the diamond broker installed," he rambled on, "I have made my own contributions. Inside the—"

Mady stepped up and placed her hand on his arm. "I'm not going to steal it. You need to relax." She stepped back and crossed her arms, an expectant look on her face. Slowly, one foot began to tap.

"Right," Carter said. He coughed and smiled, remembering the first moment he saw her, when she made her entrance at Marsten Hall. At that time he only knew she was beautiful and he was filled with the normal red-blooded male thoughts of "show me yours, and I'll show you mine."

This is not what I had in mind.

Behind him, the tapping foot increased in tempo, bringing him back to the moment. He entered a second code into a small keypad. "I added an infrared eye to the inside of the safe. Anyone disturbing the interior without disabling the infrared scan will set off multiple alarms."

The foot tapped a little faster.

He reached in and removed a heavy wood box of ebony and inlaid ivory chased with a gold bead. He walked to the center of the room, setting the box on a table.

She came to his side and waited as he manipulated the clasp on the front of the box. He raised the lid and retrieved a brilliant red silk-covered box. The top of the box came off and he pulled out a yellow embroidered silk bag. He opened the bag—and the real Egyptian coin tumbled out.

It sparkled in his palm, alive and commanding, waiting.

She stared, frozen, her mouth pursed in concentration. Suddenly she jerked and gasped. "Cripes, Carter, I thought you'd never get to the bottom of your little maze of boxes." She exhaled loudly, making the air whistle through her lips. Her eyes fixed on the coin and she took it. Before she could move, he stopped her, curling his hands around hers.

"Examine it to your heart's content," he said. "I'm going upstairs to change. Is there anything you need before I go?"

She shook her head. "All I want is to see the coin." She looked at him, gratitude in her eyes. "You're leaving it with me," she said, smiling tentatively. "I promise to keep it safe."

"There is no one else I trust with it." He moved the empty boxes to the floor and turned on the table lamp. When she was all settled, he headed for the door to go upstairs. Looking back over his shoulder, he saw she was absorbed in her examination. He breathed a great sigh of relief.

At last, he thought, *someone worthy, someone who isn't afraid.* Before rounding the corner he called out, "There's a glass in the drawer."

Mady looked up in time to catch a glimpse of Carter's broad back before he disappeared from her view. She hefted the coin, feeling its solid weight. She relaxed; so far all was well. She pulled out her velvet bag. Removing her coin, she held it up and read, *"You are the Children of Gods."* She spoke defiantly, demanding the genie-of-all-mysteries to reveal the meaning of this cryptic phrase.

The words rolled off her tongue, making her feel good as she spoke them. Even though she had not one single clue of the statement's meaning, she kept her lips clamped together, refusing to give energy to anything remotely negative. She cocked her head to one side and closed her eyes, soliciting answers.

Nothing happened.

"Hmmm." She pressed on, reading the Egyptian coin. "Find your Power within the Greatest Temple." She cocked her head again—waiting, listening, receptive.

Nothing happened.

She placed the coins side by side and examined them with and without the magnifying glass, and still she knew nothing. She frowned and clamped her lips in concentration. All her thoughts screamed and clamored for answers, yet none came.

Sheer desperation made her threaten, "All right then, I command you, reveal to me who left you behind and why." She squinted and lifted the corner of one lip, growling.

Nothing happened.

She relaxed her face into a new pose—one of beseeching humility. "Three couture gowns, and my ... first-born, uh, grandchild, if you will please tell me how and why you are here."

Her breath locked in her lungs, she waited, receptive to any spontaneous, brilliant insightful discovery that would lead her to answers, but no epiphany came. "Ooohhh," she moaned, throwing her hands in the air, scowling with frustration. "Damn. What am I missing?"

"So that's the secret."

Mady looked up and saw Carter lounging against the door to the library. He had changed into jeans and a light sweater.

He said, "All you have to do is talk to them. I would have never thought of that," he teased. "How brilliant you are, Mady."

"Carter, don't tease me. Cripes," she exclaimed, pulling her shoulders up in frustration. "When I had just one artifact, it made me as mad as a hatter." She poked her finger at one of the coins on the table. "But now that my prayers have been answered and I have two artifacts," she said, stabbing the other coin, "I am now twice as mad—" *Stab, stab.* "—and I still don't have any answers."

She sighed with frustration. "What ... what, what am I missing?" She ran her finger around the edge of one coin, touching each individual symbol. "I believe the circle is a complete alphabet—none of the symbols repeat. But your coin—I hoped for more of a clue. Instead, all I have are more questions. Tell me your story now, how did you come by this artifact?"

Carter pulled a chair to her side. He picked up his coin and rubbed it between his palms. "My Uncle Arthur was another Carter with his heart in Egypt—but he was a scholar and an archivist, not a digger. His greatest joy was to stay in the museum library, surrounded by the artifacts of Egypt and their documentation, filling countless hours recording and postulating.

"The doctors in England told him to find a drier climate, and he said, 'Right oh,' packed for Egypt and was gone within the month. He settled in Cairo and spent his life there working in the archaeological community. He became quite the expert and was admired and respected for his extensive studies.

"Over the years he became a good friend of Ibrahim Hassan, curator at the Egyptian Museum in Cairo. Those two would spend hours with their heads together over that horrid Turkish coffee, comparing their notes and ideas.

"One day Ibrahim took Uncle into the old storerooms where they kept the pieces not on display. He had something special he wanted Arthur to see, in hopes that his good friend might understand it. It was an oopart, unidentified and entirely unexplainable."

The excitement fired in Mady and she squirmed in her seat.

Carter said, "The coin was discovered inside the royal ship of Khufu when it was excavated from the pit on the south side of the Great Pyramid. It was found in a jewel-crusted box, placed amid the disassembled pieces of the boat like a present left to be discovered and opened. Because of its mystery, it was set aside and put into storage. You know how they are, nothing unexplained is allowed."

Mady nodded. "Yeah, yeah, evidence that doesn't match the theory." She waved her hands. "Go on."

"Uncle took the coin without documentation. Ibrahim simply handed it to him and said, 'Check it out old boy. Bring it back when you are finished.'

"The next day Uncle learned that just hours after he took the artifact, Ibrahim's body was found floating in the Nile. He was murdered, his tongue severed. He bled to death. On his wrists were ligature marks where he had been bound. The news of the murder was not made public.

"My uncle was horrified. He believed the brutal murder of his good friend was somehow connected to the artifact that he now possessed illegally. Fearing for his life, he left Egypt that day. He came home and told no one about it until he lay on his deathbed."

"I was always Arthur's favorite, as we shared this love of Egypt." Carter looked past her to the windows, now dark with night, the city lights a haze in the fog. "He gave me the artifact, telling the story with his last breaths, the tears for his dear friend pouring—"

Carter's voice stuttered, but he continued. " 'Be afraid, Alex,' Arthur said. 'Be very afraid, tell no one about the artifact.' "

Carter paused to clear his throat and roll his shoulders. "That was in 2010. I investigated the curator's murder. His death remains a cold case. Also, when his relatives came to collect Ibrahim's cremated remains, they found that someone else had come in and taken them, claiming to be the family." He frowned and shrugged. "Only an outsider would do such a thing. A theft like that just doesn't happen."

While his shrug pretended unconcern, creases of worry crowded his eyes. "Then I did a little research on the symbols and discovered that they are not duplicated as a whole or individually anywhere in recorded history. I am certain they are ... unearthly, as you call them.

"Since acquiring the coin I have been on a silent search for other ooparts with the symbols. Like you, I thought other coins would bring answers. Until tonight and meeting you," he said, "I have been unsuccessful."

He grinned weakly and ran a hand through his hair. "Well, they say confession is good for the soul and I agree. It does feel good to tell someone. Within the darkness of its mystery, the damn thing has been a compelling entity. As you mentioned earlier in the car ... I believe you know what that feels like."

His words sank into the chilling quiet that surrounded them. A clock booming in the background sounded like grenades exploding down the street.

Mady squeezed her eyes shut and shivered, clutching Carter's hand. "Sorry, I just had a vision of him—Ibrahim—in the mud." She shook like a wet dog and rolled her shoulders. "Carter, I know everyone is afraid of these artifacts, but honestly, how certain are we these crimes are connected to the coins?"

Carter stared out at the night, taking his time to answer. When he spoke, his voice was deep and his words chilling.

"Better to err on the side of caution and live to laugh about it."

He looked at her and delivered his next words with

piercing and deliberate emphasis. "You know what proving your theory would do to the world. Understanding that should scare the hell out of you."

She nodded, her face filled with sadness. "And yet this," she said, shaking the coin. "This should eclipse everything. It kills me not to go public, but I agree with you and my mother, that your caution has merit."

She put her hands on his arm and held a tight grip. "My instincts tell me there is something critically important in all of this. If we are in danger, that makes understanding the symbols all the more imperative." She exhaled, deflated, and rubbed at her scalp with her fingers, raking them through her hair. "Just when I think I'm on the brink of a discovery—now I have more questions than ever." Fatigue and frustration pulled at her eyes. "So, what do we do now?"

"I'm not sure," he answered. "It's late, and it's been a rather intense evening. Will you forgive me if I tell you I'm famished? Would you like to get something to eat?" He shrugged one hopeless shoulder. "I'm afraid we'll have to go out. I don't cook much."

Mady wrinkled her nose. "After the vision I just had—" She glanced at the night-filled windows and shook her head. "But I don't want to go back to my hotel room with my mind full of these pictures. There is an all night place near my hotel where we can eat. Maybe that is a good idea." She stood and asked, "Before we go, I'd like to splash some cold water on my face. Which way is the—?"

"Just outside the library, around the corner, first door on the left," Carter said. "I'll reset the security system and meet you in the hallway. You'll be all right, won't you?"

"I'm fine," she said. "It takes more than an awful story to derail me. Go fiddle with your electronics and I'll see you at the door. I'm taking my coin. I don't like leaving it anywhere, not even here in your house with all of its security."

He picked up the coins and pocketed his duplicate and original before handing Mady's Sumerian coin to her with the velvet bag. She paused for a quick scrutiny of the coin, giving Carter a sheepish glance.

"I would probably do the same," he volunteered.

Mady snorted with humor and nodded, seeing he understood. She put the coin in its velvet case and slid the precious bag into the zippered front pocket of her jeans. "I'll just be a minute," she said and left the room.

Carter returned the various boxes that housed his coin to the safe and reset the false bookcase. Still feeling the effects of the curator's story, he went to a special panel by the library door. There, beneath a sliding door, several electronic display lights indicated the status of his multiple security systems.

God bless the diamond broker.

In the interest of keeping his business deals private, the broker installed, along with the false bookcase and its safe, an expensive in-house system of electronic counter-measures. Initially, Carter laughed when the sales agent showed him the extensive equipment.

Since acquiring the coin, he didn't laugh any more. He was grateful for the added security measures. "Come on, old boy," he chided. "You're as bad as the diamond broker."

To prove the curator's story had no effect, he slid back the panel door. "See," he said with satisfaction, "there is nothing amiss." He slid the door back into place and took one step before he stopped mid-stride. He twisted to stare at the little door, his breath caught in his throat.

What did I just see?

It's not possible, he thought, running a hand through his hair. But there, on the bottom row, a single red light had blinked in warning. That light meant only one thing.

His home was bugged.

CHAPTER FOUR

1:30 AM
London

Faces, so many faces to remember ...

Jack Greer stared out the glass windows of his corner office, scowling and thrumming his fingers against his desk.

The One. His face you don't live to talk about.

In his mind, Greer saw Maelstrom and the events of their last meeting. Their exchange was intense and contentious, and the effects of the rippling fear had been too much, even for Greer. He had gone straight home afterward to wash off the stink of his sweat and change his clothes.

There is no escape. No one is beyond The One's reach.

The enormous room Greer oversaw bore the evidence of that. Beyond the glass windows of his office was row after row of data storage containing sensitive information going back decades. The files might involve an individual, a corporation, or an entire government. Presidents, Popes, physicists, astronomers, archaeologists, rich people, rebels and royalty.

Those who interested The One comprised a long and complex list. There were so many lives, so many faces—

"Jack, you look like hell. Do you ever sleep?"

Greer straightened and stared at the young technician standing before him with a spreadsheet in his hand. "Yeah, thanks for the concern. What do you have?"

"It's just a flag, in town. Here—"

In an instant, Greer's heart skidded to a stop. He didn't want to deal with any flags and he didn't want to know what was in the spreadsheet.

No, no—more than anything, he did not want—

The kid held out the report. Greer's arms refused to rise and take it. Instead, he pushed his chair back, eyes fixed on the spreadsheet like it was a basket of snakes.

"Whatever, man," the kid said. He dropped the sheets on the desk and walked out, muttering and shaking his head.

Greer stared at the pages splayed out before him. His heart had jumped from a stall to a drum roll, driving sweat to pepper his armpits. He heard his office door close, distant and far away, beyond the pounding in his ears.

It's just a bunch of numbers, no need to panic ...

"No, it isn't just a bunch—" he began, but his voice faded out. When he spoke again, his speech was mechanical as he droned on, quoting directly from his operations manual. "It's a statistical improbability assessment generated by an anomaly requiring the assignment of such men or equipment as are necessary to determine answers to the questions created ... by the anomaly," he finished softly.

A slow chill poured down his spine and pooled around his rear, shrinking his rectum. "And sooner or later," he whispered, "—the numbers will become faces." He clamped his lips together and nodded with the certainty of a seer.

And the faces end up in your dreams.

He bolted from his thoughts and snatched up the spreadsheet, swinging his chair around to his computer. He typed in the encrypted numbers and waited, his fingers rapping on the desk in a race with his heart as a deep well of dread hardened in him. Too quickly, the seconds passed as electronic bytes churned through cyberspace, bringing him names and faces.

While the file printed, he glanced over his shoulder through the glass windows of his office. No one watched. He wiped his hands on his pants and whispered a prayer before picking up the completed file. All through the brief prayer he winced, knowing he had no right to anything divine. Still, he prayed for his condemned future—and for the many faces out there that he knew waited for him.

He scanned the file quickly, his muscles clenched all the while, as if he were flying above a minefield. When he got to the names, his knowing heart slammed into his ribs with growing trepidation.

"Oh no," he moaned.

I recognize these names.

Drawing a deep breath, he forced himself to re-read the information and focus on the pictures. Sluggish memories stirred in his miserable brain until the dread seeped into his bones. "Aagghh … nooo."

I know these faces. I have touched these people.

Worthless denial was always bitter. While he couldn't place the full details, he knew he had altered these people's lives in some way during his long career.

He hunched his shoulders again and rubbed his neck.

Now there would be new faces in his dreams.

He let his head fall into his hands. Inside, a relentless wash of remorse blistered his core. Disgust, for himself and for his future, was an old, well-picked scab on his soul. He lifted his head to gaze out at the sea of surveillance data surrounding him and knew there was a file somewhere marked *Jack Greer.*

Perhaps Maelstrom knew about the land Greer bought in Oregon. He had paid cash and gave his buddy Steve the authorization to put the property in his own name. Just in case.

Fool, you'll never escape.

"Oh, screw it," he said, slamming his palm down on the photos. Growling, he grabbed the phone and dialed. While the number rang, he flipped the photos over and pushed them across the desk.

He had seen enough.

"Bennett, it's Greer, get your shoes on, buddy—I got a job for you. I want you to pick up a chip. Your mark is a blonde in a swanky neighborhood. This is Level One, so just follow and report anything suspicious, but make no contact, understand?"

He rubbed the disgust from his face.

Not enough sleep, pushing too hard.

"Yeah, I hear you," he snapped, snarling at the disembodied voice from the receiver. "Two 'persons of interest' are playing together, and I need to know what their game is. Hurry your ugly ass over there."

Greer terminated the call. *With any luck,* he thought, *this little affair will be put to rest without incident.* He heaved a sigh of relief and managed half a grin … albeit with little conviction.

"No need to disturb Maelstrom," he whispered quietly.

•

A Secluded Residence Outside Paris

Trapped as sure as an animal in a cage. How I hate this place and these people.

Maelstrom sighed, his disappointment an old companion. In his chest a threatening rumble stirred and he turned around, having reached the end of his circuit. Pacing was his habit, and he had seen many fine carpets reduced to threads beneath his feet.

His great strides took him back and forth across the old war room of his French chateau. He stopped at one of the narrow slits in the wall and touched the cool stone. Its coarseness scratched the thick pads on his fingertips, sparking memories.

These ancient stones are as cold and unforgiving as I am. We have survived the centuries, yet neither of us is immortal.

The window was a slit once used by archers in the defense of the chateau. He smiled, fondly remembering those exciting times. Glancing over his shoulder at his brother, he asked, "What happened to the spirit of those brave men who dared to hold their keep by such means? Do you remember how fierce they were? They fought us with bows and arrows."

He shook his head and laughed, a short barking sound. "In spite of their crude abilities, they were opponents worth fighting. Such spirit deserved respect."

Making a sound that boiled with menace and angst, he turned from the window abruptly. However primitive the human species had been, however spineless they had become, it appeared they would survive him in the end.

But all wasn't finished yet.

His solitary audience, the only other remaining survivor of his species, was a reminder that filled Maelstrom with sorrow for those of his kind who had passed. Once a powerful brotherhood—gods to many of the people of this planet—their meager group was reduced to just the two of them.

So be it, he thought. As long as he drew breath, all plans will continue and dominion will be established. He shrugged his massive shoulders. Someone had to be at the top.

It might as well be me, regardless of how long I have left.

Like his namesake, he was a mad vortex rearranging all in his path to suit his plans. Denied his single greatest desire—escape from his fate on this planet—he was an endless source of angst in motion. He never wanted to live here ... and he refused to die here. Yet for all his wealth and power, he remained trapped.

He growled and flexed his great hands, curling the fingers into tremendous fists. Waves of power and anger rolled off him until he relaxed, bringing his focus back to his earlier ranting.

"I told you it would be easy," he said, striding back to the table where his brother sat silent. "They are as fat and stupid as cows," he snarled. "I have seen it a thousand times on every continent and in every culture since we came to this planet."

He continued to pace, unable to keep still.

"Look what happened to that last generation that 'fought for freedom.' They were subverted with greed, the fools. Ten years of a bull market and they were quickly addicted to the good life." He sneered and his deep rumbling voice curdled with disgust.

"Do you hear them cry for peace, love and freedom now?" he asked. He coughed and his lip lifted, exposing one fang. "The only thing they weep for now is their money."

Lost in the storm of his thoughts, he strode back and forth, a whirlwind of energy. Suddenly, he noticed it—the subtle odor of decay coming from his last brother—a scent he knew all too well signaled the beginning of the end for that one. The stiff hairs on the back of Maelstrom's neck stirred and he softly inhaled. He gave a slanted glance to his brother.

Soon he will be gone, and I'll be the last.

Pretending not to have noticed, he returned to his tirade. "We have reduced them—weakened their bodies by poisoning their food, and fragmented their attentions with multiple non-stop conflicts. Their world is cascading into my control in spite of their spirit, what could have been their only salvation. Fortunately for us, their greed stifled their spirit."

He snarled, and slammed his mighty fist on the table.

Where would I be, if not for a meteor shower?

Such thoughts were ultimately worthless. He shook his head, weary with his rage and regret, and continued pacing, needing a vent for his fierce anger. Trapped on this primitive planet, his manipulations of power and politics were all he had.

Some consolation came in the form of his success.

"They are virtually powerless against us," he sneered. "Even if they had a power, someone would try to steal it or sell it. Their sightless drive to consume every last resource on the planet will serve to be their ultimate downfall if I don't take over.

"Soon, those lackeys in Brussels will initiate the final *coup de grâce* to freedom—a microchip embedded in the new currency after the old system is brought down. Once that happens, which is well on its way thanks to that special greed called derivatives, humanity's precious freedom is finished."

An air of satisfaction emanated from his large face. He leaned back and smirked, waving one great paw in a sad and final salute. "May their squandered lives and souls be damned."

He gestured to the map of Europe on the wall. "I'm considering what to do with the boys in Brussels." Tapping the desk in thought, he said, "The bankers are wise to fear the Amun-ra. Turning them over to those ancient jackals should prove entertaining."

A spine-chilling smile crossed his visage as he leaned forward. "You ask me, why? Why do I persist with my desire to dominate these little people? How am I able to achieve my goals?" He grinned with obvious delight, eager for his own answer.

"Because they allow it," he announced.

His point succinctly made, he sat back. "Nonetheless, one could almost feel sorry for them," he added lightly. "For when did they have a chance against us?"

He bared his teeth with pleasure, exposing the tips of his fang teeth in a parody of laughter. Air wheezed through his nasal passages and created a sound that skittered across nerves. Finally his great shoulders shook with humor as he threw his head back.

"Ah, my little pets. You were so easy."

•

2:00 AM
London
Mayfair

Henri parked the Rolls within sight of the garage exit to Carter's apartment building. From his vantage point two blocks away, he could see lights come on in a second floor room with large windows.

He shifted, restless in his driver's seat. Even though the hour was late, he knew better than to ask how long they would maintain this watch. He moved again, stretching his legs out before him, seeking comfort. Minutes passed and the boring stillness of surveillance settled around them once again.

St. Germain's voice came softly across the open intercom. "Being the hunter is no easier than being the prey, is it? Stay sharp, I feel a long night is before us."

•

In his library, Carter heard Mady's distant voice through the buzzing in his ears.

"Carter?" she called. "Are you coming or not? I thought you were going to feed me. What are you doing?"

He stood rigidly still, rationalizing his concern over the blinking red security light.

Why is this light activated?

Mady entered the library. He gave her a sharp, troubled look. It didn't take long for her to reach his side. She placed her hand on his arm and searched his stricken face. "What?" she asked. She followed his gaze and squeezed his arm, shaking him to break the spell. "Hey, what is it? You're spooking me."

"This can't be right," he said. He walked to the security panel and slid the door open, revealing the blinking red light that disturbed him. "This red light tells me a transmission is being broadcast from inside this apartment. But I don't understand how, since all the other systems are green. If there hasn't been a break in, then how is there a transmission from inside?"

Frowning, he stepped back and looked around, wanting to understand, wanting this to be something other than what was screeching at him from the back of his mind. He walked to a closet and returned with a shiny aluminum case, placing it on the same table where they sat and talked earlier. The case contained a wand-like device attached to a small, hand held meter. He adjusted the controls and checked the numbers, then took the device to the windows.

He paced in an ever-widening pattern while watching the glowing numbers. After three hesitant passes, he looked from the device to Mady, his expression blank even though adrenaline flowed hot and bitter across his nerves.

Eyes locked onto hers, he walked ahead, pointing the wand at her. He visually searched her up and down as he approached, looking for something to calm the shrieking suspicion in his mind. But she carried no bag or jacket with pockets; there was no place to hide a cell phone or any other device. In truth, her jeans were so tight he could see the velvet bag in her zippered front pocket.

Hesitant, he lifted his gaze to her face. Her blue eyes were huge against the pale of her cheeks. Wetting his lips, he said, "Madelyn, it's you. The transmission is coming from you."

Her eyes expanded and her mouth fell open. "Carter," she said, frowning as she pulled the contents from her rear pockets. "I have my passport and a handful of pound notes." She showed him, patting down her pockets for emphasis. "See, there's nothing here. Check again, your equipment is off."

He could see she carried nothing, yet he knew the equipment was in perfect working order. So that meant—

"Carter, I said your—"

"No, it's not the equipment," he said. "There's something on you." He frowned and stepped toward her. She stood silent, shaking her head back and forth, but he had to know what alerted the security. He took another step and cringed inside for what he had to do.

At a distance of three feet a new light on the meter came to life, this one increasing in tempo as he neared her. He waved the receiver up and down from her face to her toes and the light pulsed faster. Moving around behind her, he waved the receiver at her backside, watching the meter, as the pulsing became a steady light.

"Raise your shirt. Let me see your back, just below the shoulder blade on your right side." He spoke without inflection, afraid of startling her.

Mady stood with a rigid spine as she reached back and lifted her sweater to expose her shoulder blades. "This is silly ... it's not possible," she protested. "You can look all you want, but there is nothing to see. Check the battery on your stupid little light." She laughed and choked. "When you sort this out," she finished, regaining her composure. "We'll have a good chuckle about how silly we are. You know, telling a scary story and getting the willies."

Carter saw her expression from across her shoulder, and recognized her need for confirmation this was a mistake. But he couldn't give it to her. He lingered, staring at her back. "Breathe, Mady, breathe."

She whispered, barely audible. "I was waiting to hear, hear you say it was just the battery. There has to be some mistake," she sobbed, clenching her fists.

Carter continued to gaze, lost in the sublime beauty of her back, remembering how the sight of her bare back affected him earlier when he unzipped her gown. Her skin was flawless, the color of ivory with a touch of summer sun. The texture was fine, and begged for his touch with the song of the siren. Like golden peaches, her perfection made his mouth water. He swallowed, terrified at what he might discover, of what he might have to do to that beautiful back.

"Say something, please," she said. "You're killing me."

He cleared his throat, producing a ragged cough. Trying to keep his voice steady, he asked, "There's a small scar here, just below the blade. Tell me about it."

"Oh," she deflated with a 'whoosh' of air and a great sigh. "That's nothing. I fell off a horse; there was a small laceration and they stitched it up. It's just a little scar, that's all."

He set the equipment on the floor and probed her back with the tip of one finger, poking around beneath her shoulder blade.

She pitched her head forward, letting her chin hang toward her chest, her arms clasped in a defensive posture. She hunched forward, as though protecting her front from what was happening on her back.

"Where did you have this riding accident, and who stitched it up for you?" He stepped around in front of her and reached down to lift her chin.

Answering with her eyes squeezed tight, her whisper was so soft, he could barely hear.

"It was a couple months after my parents ... my first birthday alone. I was here in England, at Sir Roger's country estate. He called and insisted I come over and stay with him. He even bought my ticket from New York as part of my birthday present. I was glad for the opportunity to get away.

"He had a little get-together that weekend in my honor. We rode on Sunday morning, and the mare I was on startled a hare from the brush, which, of course, frightened the mare. She dumped me in front of everyone. I landed in brush and got all scraped up."

She paused to roll her head from side to side. Carter's heart went out to her when her gravel-filled voice continued.

"I thought it was nothing, but Sir Roger wanted one of his other guests, a doctor, to take a look at it. I don't remember the man's name. He was a friend of Roger's and that was enough for me. I forgot all about it."

Carter reached out to grab hold of her arms. Her eyes were still tightly clenched, so he shook her gently, needing to see the goddess power in those beautiful blue eyes.

"There is something there, under your skin. What do you want to do?" He spoke slowly.

Her face blanched and she scrunched it up, panting and fighting for control. He stroked her arms, wanting to help her, yet unsure of what to do. He knew what he would want if the decision were his.

Finally, she took a deep ragged breath and color flooded back into her cheeks. When she opened her eyes, a nuclear blaze simmered in the glittering blue depths.

He let go of her and stepped back.

Through clenched teeth, she ground out, "If your equipment is not faulty, and you are completely certain in your suspicions, then I want you to get something sharp and remove whatever is there. And I want you to do it now!"

Carter saw the goddess return, with a vengeance. He jumped up immediately and collected the items he needed, returning to spread everything out on the table: cotton, alcohol, scalpel, tweezers, antibiotic cream, and bandages. She looked at what he brought and shivered when she saw the scalpel.

"From my field supplies," he said. "I keep them close at hand. One never knows ... " His words faded as he realized the shocking truth in those three simple words.

He grabbed a solid hardback chair and pulled it to the table. She turned and sat, giving him her back. With no concern for modesty, she pulled her bra and sweater up and over her head. Clutching them to her chest, she leaned forward and placed her chin on top of the chair back. "Thank God you are here. Just get it out."

When he applied alcohol to her back, the skin raised up in goose bumps. Carter looked from the satin of her back to the scalpel he held poised ready, and sent a quick silent prayer. He brought the razor edge to her back. "Steady now."

•

Two blocks away, Solomon and Henri waited patiently in the limousine.

Henri looked at his watch, noting the hour at a little past two o'clock. London being a workingman's town, the streets were empty. Most of the clubs were closed and the tourists snug in their hotel beds.

The quiet night reminded him of a story Grandpere told when he and Solomon were boys. The details were long forgotten, but he recalled how evil preferred to do its business in the late night hours, when man was farthest from the light of day and most afraid.

He remembered how he and Solomon, just little boys, shrank back, eyes huge and frightened. But Grandpere wagged his great eyebrows and made a funny face so that they burst into giggles. He loved the dear old man as much as Solomon, and wished Grandpere were here now with those big bushy brows to help them face the dark fears.

The night had been deserted for some time when a late model Renault came slowly down the street. Henri watched with interest. "I believe we have company," he called softly. "A Renault is taking up a position closer in."

"The night gets crowded, does it not?" St. Germain said. "I wonder what Mr. Carter and his lady friend have done to attract so much attention? This does not change our plans. We will stay far enough back to escape the notice of the Renault.

"If the Jaguar reappears, let this intruder take the lead. Can you see the license plate? Let's see who else is interested in our unsuspecting, yet popular friends."

•

Bennett parked the Renault so he could see the entryway to the fancy apartment building matching the address Greer gave him. He looked at the file, an abridged version containing only what he needed— photos, a name and address, habits and a list of family members and social contacts.

"Anthropology and archaeology," he read. "Hmmm. Two little diggers scratching around together. What have you kiddies found?"

He yawned. It looked to be another long night lurking around after two unsuspecting idiots. He studied the photos for the first time.

"Well, at least the blonde's a hottie."

He gave the photo a serious perusal. *Yes*, he thought, *she is definitely a hottie.* "Maybe this won't be so boring after all," he said. He had always wanted to talk to one of those long-legged model broads. The quality of woman he got to spend time with had about half the leg this one had.

Another look at the runway photo and he felt himself grow hard. He chuckled, thinking about Greer's orders to make no contact. "Sure, Greer, I promise," he said, rubbing himself.

He settled in with anticipation, an ugly man with an ugly smile.

•

Mady breathed a sigh of relief as Carter applied antibiotic ointment to the wound on her back. Next came the comfort of a snug bandage, ending the ordeal of having her body invaded. On the table beside her lay the item of offense. Within her heart was an inconsolable rage over having been treated no better than a stock animal.

She looked at the RFID chip—a small bloody piece the size of a grain of rice. Lodged under her shoulder blade, it was no wonder she had not detected its presence. She drained a snifter of brandy and placed the glass on the table next to the chip. Behind her, Carter fussed, hovering around her.

"There you go, all tidied up. Are you all right now? Would you like another brandy?" His voice rattled on, betraying his nervousness and making her smile.

He walked around the chair and kneeled down to peer at her. His voice was husky with emotion. "I've long been an admirer of the strength of women. I can't say that I would have been so composed, were it me. What do you want to do now?"

"Carter, you're babbling, you know, and you can stop fussing, too, because I'm fine … now that this thing is out of me."

She stared at the chip and was surprised when her stomach lurched in a sickening wave. Her mouth watered and she swallowed hard, daring her stomach to misbehave.

"No … I am fine," she repeated, but her voice quivered, sounding uncertain. She looked up at Carter, her face feeling numb and pasty, somehow not her own. She started to speak, shut her mouth, and then opened it again. *Great*, she thought, *now I'm gaping like a grounded fish.* She slumped forward, drained and fatigued. "I don't know … I have no idea what to do. Give me a minute to think."

She sat with her hands relaxed in her lap, not even a foot moved. She closed her eyes and slowed her breathing, shutting down … going still … a lost boy scout alone in the woods.

Until one white-hot emotion came clear in her mind.

I will kill whoever did this to me.

Abruptly she turned around in the chair to examine the thing Carter cut from her back. The bloody chip sat on one of his brilliant white handkerchiefs, as alarming as a snake at a birthday party.

She poked at it. "I'm horrified and I want to hide, but I don't know which way to run. I'm outraged, and I want to deliver vengeance upon someone, but I don't know which way to turn. The only thing I am sure of is—I'm glad I have you with me tonight."

He moved a chair opposite her and they sat knee to knee. He took her chilled hands in his. "Do you have any reason to suspect Sir Roger knew about your mother's coin? You say she never told him about it?"

She shook her head. "If he knew, he didn't learn it from my mother. According to her journal, she never mentioned it to anyone, not even my father. My mother was very intuitive, something I inherited from her. Maybe Sir Roger started giving her the creeps, like he did with me." She threw him a sideways glance. "That inner voice, I might add, expressed no objections to telling you."

"Of course," he beamed. "I was the right one to tell." He squeezed her hands and drew his eyebrows together in mock ferociousness. He looked so silly, she laughed and felt better.

"There was a scandal surrounding the Marsten name just after the war," Carter said. "When I was a young boy I remember hearing my uncles argue about it, still titillated by the scandal decades after the fact. It was all about the Marsten family fortune. Apparently, where there once had been none, suddenly there was a great deal. The mystery generated tremendous debate.

"This is when the gold lion's crest was added to the gates of Marsten Hall. No public explanation was ever made about the significance of the lion's head, or the cause of their reversal of family fortune." He gazed past her, lost in memory.

Mady smiled and squeezed his hands, bringing him back. "Thank you for stopping me from talking to Sir Roger. I know he's involved in this in someway." She shuddered, feeling as if an evil eye tracked her. "God only knows what they would have done to me that weekend if I hadn't accommodated them by falling off my horse."

Suddenly the hurt and betrayal surged in, wrapping around her, drowning her. "Carter," she sobbed, "I feel so violated. To have this done to me at the hands of someone I trusted is—"

She choked and her voice cracked as she searched for the words. "First, my parents ... and the artifact. Now, that thing," she said, nodding at the handkerchief's evil contents. She struggled to speak through the tremors rattling her teeth. Chills swept through her body until she shuddered violently. Carter moved toward her, sympathy in his eyes, but she raised her hand.

"No," she commanded, stopping him with the tone of her voice. She shook, not with distress, but with anger. "I want to know who did this to me. All my life I have respected the rights of every living thing. Even the ancient remains I handle are accorded the highest degree of respect."

Angst roiled within and crumpled her composure. She grabbed Carter's hands, squeezing with crushing strength, sinking her fingernails into his flesh. "Dammit, there are some things you just don't do," she cried. "Every life is born with an inviolate reverence—period. I have been stripped of that regard. I have been treated like a thing, as though I had no dominion over my own body, and I hate that."

Her eyes brimmed with tears but she fought for control, refusing to let them fall. "I'm not finished with whoever is responsible for this."

She crushed the anger and the tears that threatened. *One, two, three,* she counted. Slowly, she sat up and rubbed her face and smoothed her hair. Again she poked at the device on the table, pushing it around before suddenly snatching it up.

"It's a tracking chip. Someone has been recording my whereabouts for three years. Who? Why this kind of surveillance? This is no dime store device. To broadcast, it has to be very high-tech ... and very expensive. Who could do this?"

Carter offered no answer, and her questions hung in the air—pointing always in the same direction.

The coins.

She stood up and collected the chip with the bloody handkerchief. "Let's go. I'm ready to eat."

All the way back to town, she silently simmered. Emotion and fatigue came rushing in, adding to her anger and inflaming her outrage even further. "Yes, those responsible have not seen the last of me," she said in a sudden burst. Her ragged voice and the sudden words grated harsh against the silence in the Jaguar.

Carter eyed her and pulled a mock face of horror, making her cheeks fill with heat.

"Well, how would you feel?" she demanded. "If someone put a tracking device in your body without your permission—you'd be pissed, too."

Her voice shook and she turned toward the window. "Sorry, I'm just having a little trouble with all this. I mean, a few hours ago I was wearing Armani and ready to take on the world."

She gazed solemnly out the window, her chin on her palm. "Now I want to kill someone—" She shrugged, shattered and baffled.

"I know you feel—" he said.

"I'm outraged—" she blurted. She turned to explain further, but his grim expression cut her short.

"Exactly," he hissed. "However, until we know a little more about what we're dealing with, I wouldn't be in such a hurry to deliver this vengeance. Someone else could get killed."

Mady sat back and clutched Carter's jacket around her shoulders. She knew he was right to urge caution. But the desire for retribution was a living force—now a part of her, filling the void left in her flesh by the chip's extraction.

All action creates an equal and opposite reaction.

"This doesn't change anything. I won't be stopped," she said. "Not by them, not by anyone. The symbols will change everything we know about life on this planet."

She felt her passion for the coin catch fire, bringing hot and cold waves. "A change for the human race that is long overdue," she declared, "and I intend to see it happens."

They found the restaurant near her hotel, clean and quiet, serving American breakfast all night long. Carter parked on the street and they walked to the front door.

"Deano's Diner?" he asked, lifting one questioning eyebrow.

"Hey," she said with a knowing smirk. "At this hour in London, beggars can't be choosy. Besides, Deano's Diner has a unique feature. This part of the building was a bank during the 1800s. The women's bathroom is in the old vault. You could have a heck of a party in there." She grinned, her blue eyes enticing. "Besides, the food is excellent."

They walked into the smell of hot coffee and fried potatoes, soliciting a loud rumble from Mady's stomach. She led Carter to a table in the corner, cautiously eyeballing the other customers as her sense of violation came rushing back. Who would know about her tracking chip? Was there someone here in this room that could be following the chip's beacon? She hated this feeling of being watched.

She waved to the waitress and gave a runway smile. Squeezing Carter's hand as they slid into a booth, she told him, "You're right about thinking better on a full stomach."

The waitress arrived and Mady ordered before Carter could open the menu. "Bring us a number three," she said. "Make that with bacon, eggs scrambled and wheat toast. Also two omelets—one veggie, one with meat; an order of the blueberry crepes, a side of fresh fruit, and—"

As Carter listened, his eyebrows lifted by degrees with every item she ordered, causing her to laugh out loud. She smothered her chuckles long enough to add, "—and an order of that French toast Dean makes with Frangelica."

•

Outside Deano's Diner, Bennett parked away from the Jag, yet within view of the front door of the restaurant. It was now 3:15 AM and he regretted loosing sight of the blonde and her companion when they entered the eatery.

Standard procedure was for him to remain where he

was, but he was toying with the idea of going in and having breakfast. She didn't know she was being followed, and no one at his office would find out if he went in. Besides, if she slipped out a back door, he'd never know it from out here.

He looked at the photo one more time and made up his mind. While he wanted to see her close up ... much closer, the prospect of having biscuits and gravy was irresistible. Sending caution to hell, he said, "Oh, baby, I'm coming in." He checked his watch, waited ten minutes, then got out and walked into the restaurant.

•

When the food arrived, Mady's mouth watered. "Lord, let me eat like a Viking and then get some sleep," she mumbled in prayer under her breath. She watched Carter and smothered a grin. He was pursing his lips in appreciation and mouthing "thank you" each time the waitress set down a dish. As soon as she left, he rubbed his hands together like a man going to work, picked up his fork, and declared, "Let's eat."

They fell upon the feast and gorged themselves shamelessly. The coffee, hot and strong, came from a huge thermos on the table. It didn't take long for them to empty the plates.

Mady picked at the last of the French toast and quietly eyed a man who sat at the counter. Carter chuckled, drawing her attention away.

"No wonder you ordered so much food. I didn't realize you were actually going to eat like a Viking," he said.

She grinned and offered the compliment back. "You have a healthy appetite yourself, Mister." She stretched her long legs out under the table and slouched down in her seat, leaning into him with her head on his shoulder. Now that she had eaten, she was wiped out. She groaned and rubbed her face.

"You're exhausted," he said.

She closed her eyes and pushed her nose into his neck, sniffing his scent and exhaling into him. His skin reacted with a rash of goose flesh, making her smile. "I want to sleep and wake up in another life," she whispered.

He moved his lips close to her ear, speaking softly. "I watched you at Marsten Hall, you know."

"Yes, and that was the first time you made me mad."

"No, not then, before ... in the grand salon. You seemed to have, um, some distress."

"Ah, the dress," she said, pulling back to look at him. "Yes, sitting in that gown presents certain problems."

She smiled sweetly and moved closer again, as though they were lovers sharing secrets. This time when her breath hit his neck, he picked up her hand. He stroked her palm with his thumb, making light circles in her flesh. She relaxed and sighed, content to enjoy the moment.

"Yes, you were fidgeting," he said, "very much like you have been for the last half hour—only you don't have a dress to blame it on now, do you? So, why don't you tell me what's put ants in your knickers?"

His keen observation surprised Mady, but she ignored his remark. "Shall we leave?" she asked. "I think we should catch a bus, a nice empty one. Hopefully we can find a night bus right outside."

He stopped with his hand play. "That's an excellent idea—and we shall do that, just as soon as you tell me what you're up to, Madelyn, because I know you are up to something."

She exhaled deeply, followed by a quick mumbled curse. When he reared back, eyeing her sharply at the ancient words, she used the pause to look him in the eye. With her best five-million-dollar smile, she lied through her teeth. "There is nothing wrong with my knickers." She leveled him a steady gaze. "I promise you there are no ants anywhere near me. The only thing I am up to is a full bladder."

A flicker of doubt flashed through his eyes and she pressed on. "Now, will you bring me your jacket from the car? I'll need it on the bus. I have to run to the loo, and I'll meet you outside in five. And this," she finished, pushing the bill his way with a saucy wink. "This is yours."

She held him with her best innocent expression. When she saw he was going to object, she cut him off before he could start.

"It's a public place, and I'm a big girl. I'll be fine between the loo and the front door. I'll meet you outside straight away, really, now go." She waved her hands at him in a sweeping motion.

He crossed his arms and shook his head no.

She smiled back at him, refusing to give in.

Neither one moved. Carter opened his mouth and she shook her head again. He clamped his lips together, but she could sense he was preparing to start anew.

Keeping her tone soft and guileless, she set him up. "Didn't we already discuss this part? Where you either trust me or get out? You remember that don't you?" she asked, her voice humming with the power of promise and intent. Before he could react, she moved in for the kill. Frowning as though it might be possible, she asked, "Do you need to write that down, Carter?"

He uncrossed his arms and she thought he was going to grab her and shake her like he did in his library, but he just glared. He peered into her face, squinting. "We must have a discussion about you trusting me— soon."

"On the bus, darling," she said, her smile pure cotton candy.

He stood and picked up their bill. He pointed at her like she was a naughty child. "You're up to something," he said. He leaned down so he could shake his finger in her face, but he said nothing, waving his eyebrows with recrimination.

She smiled back.

"No parties back there in the loo—" he warned.

"Aye, aye, sir. No parties, I promise." She imitated a less than perfect salute, and the corner of his mouth twitched.

He delivered a final threatening glare, working his face into a fierce and menacing scowl until she burst into laughter, drawing the attention of nearby diners. At last, he relented and gave a half-grin. With a final warning shake of his finger, he headed for the cashier.

Mady rose and walked to the rear. She knew the hallway went back and turned the corner where the men's room was on one side, with the ladies' room in the vault on the opposite side. Between the two was a public telephone.

She stopped to look back toward Carter as he paid their bill, but her eye went beyond him to the man at the counter.

While watching him earlier, she discovered he was watching them.

He didn't look like a tourist or a late night traveling

businessman. He was ugly and looked like some kind of creep that did nasty things to people for a living. Just the sight of him fired her adrenaline.

Retribution stood and screamed.

"If I'm paranoid," she spit with a huff, "it's with good reason."

A quick glance told her he watched her exit. She went down the hall. If he took the bait and followed her, she would have her proof. She slipped around the corner.

Bennett saw the couple splitting up and quickly left money on the counter for his bill. He passed Carter and they brushed shoulders as Bennett followed the blonde into the back. At the end of the hall he looked around the corner and saw the telephone. For two seconds he stood there, chewing on his lip.

I'm still within procedure, sorta.

He walked to the phone and picked up the receiver, lounging so he could see the entrance to the ladies' room on the left. Whispering a meaningless conversation, he kept the peripheral vision of one eye cast toward the door.

"Pssst."

He looked up and his whispering faltered as he froze.

There she was, in the flesh. She lifted one finger, motioning him to come with her and he stared back, stunned, unable to make his feet move.

God, what a babe.

His mouth watered and he felt himself stir.

She winked. He smiled.

He glanced back over his shoulder—they were alone, the hall empty. When he turned back, he glimpsed the curve of her hip as she retreated into the ladies' room.

It was more than he could ask. He shook his head, knowing he'd never get another opportunity like this. *What the hell*, he thought, *maybe she likes doing ugly men in public bathrooms. Whatever—I'm in.*

His ugly little grin came back and he followed her.

•

Mady burst through the restaurant door, grinning ear to ear. She met Carter at the sidewalk. One look at her flushed cheeks and his face grew stern.

"Madelyn Rose," he hissed, "what have you done?"

She glanced up the street and saw a bus approaching. "Let's go," she said, grabbing his hand.

His stern face dissolved into a grin and he chuckled. The sound was so childish Mady giggled in return. Still holding his hand, she sprinted across the intersection to the bus stop.

"Mady? What—?"

"Wait."

The bus pulled up and they darted up the steps. Mady dug her bus pass from her pocket and swiped it. Behind her, Carter's restless shifting fired her childish thrill. He squeezed her hand.

Their fares paid, she turned and ran for the back with Carter so close behind her she tripped and nearly fell, inciting a squeal and a fresh wave of breathless giggles. They reached the last row as the empty bus pulled away from the curb.

Laughing, they fell into their seats.

CHAPTER FIVE

4:00 AM
Soho

St. Germain checked his watch and stared out the limousine window.

Please God bring me some answers tonight.

"They are on the move, again, but it appears they are going for a bus," Henri called.

"Does the ugly one still follow them?"

"No. They leave without him."

St. Germain tapped his fingers. Finally, he said, "We can only hope our industrious pair will return, Henri, since Mr. Carter has left his fine automobile parked on the street. But the man from the Renault, I would like to know what has happened to him. Why don't you go to the restaurant, and bring us back something. I feel the need for a cup of coffee."

Henri got out of the Rolls, making his way to the restaurant. Soon he returned with two steaming cups and a bag of pastries for each of them.

St. Germain accepted the coffee. "What has happened to our missing fellow?" he asked. Henri passed him a bag of pastry. A puff of powdered sugar brought a smile to Solomon's lips. "Has he met with some untimely mishap?"

Henri sipped his coffee and began to chuckle. "Apparently, Mr. Carter's lady has some self-defense training. It seems the man was found lying on the floor in the ladies' toilette."

"Nooo—" St. Germain uttered, his lips puckered in a big-eyed face of mock horror. He looked up at the rear-view mirror and grinned. Sugar dusted the corners of his mouth.

"Now," Henri continued with a shrug, warming to the story, "What the man was doing in there in the first place is known only to him. However, before our lovely lady exited the diner, she informed the large Jamaican cook on duty that she had been assaulted in the loo and the culprit was in the back. She asked them to please call the police."

Henri continued with unrestrained glee, chuckling as he licked his fingers. "The cook went back and found him as she said, on the floor, barely conscious, grasping his badly mashed gonads with a broken arm. At any rate, he is locked in the refrigerator while they await the authorities."

St. Germain's laughter burst aloud before settling into smug chuckles broken by lingering guffaws. He caught Henri's look in the mirror and said, "Carter's young lady, whoever she is … sounds just delightful."

•

Jack Greer stormed from one side of his office to the other, his face contorted with disbelief. He shouted until his voice bounced off the glass walls. "You did what? She—? You're where?" He paced, one hand running through his hair. Finally, he asked, "Where is she now, Bennett?"

The answer came in a tiny voice and Greer pulled a snarling grimace. Mocking Bennett, he parroted back, "I don't know where she is. Of course you don't know, you idiot. Why? Because you're a screw-up, and now I have to fix it!"

Dammit, this isn't supposed to be happening.

Greer scrubbed at the stubble on his cheeks and closed his eyes. *Please,* he begged, *no more faces.* He closed his mind to any thoughts of the visions that plagued him and paused, trying to calm himself. He had to think straight if he wanted to stay in control.

He gripped the phone with a white-knuckled fist and growled at Bennett. "As soon as they let you out, you get in here and make your report, I don't care if you're in a bloody body cast. Is that clear? In the mean time, I want you to think about what I'm going do to you tomorrow—and make sure you strip this number from your cell phone."

What a frickin' mess.

Panting, Greer leaned against his desk. He could handle this. He could keep everyone in control and minimize damages as long as he stayed calm. But he had to fix it before another face joined the gallery in his dreams.

He made one more call. "Mason, I need you. Bennett left a mess and I need you to clean it up before something ugly gets out of the bag. You're going to pick up a mark on the loose, but she's tracked, so I'll have new coordinates for you soon. Go over to Deano's Diner on Market. Call me when you get there. Move Bennett's vehicle, and stay out of sight of the police."

Greer sat down in a huff, eyes locked in a manne-quin's fixed stare. "So much for quietly putting this inci-dent to rest," he moaned.

This was exactly the situation he wanted to avoid—field action always ended with someone getting killed. He rubbed his temples and closed his eyes. Allowing another death to join his dreams was unacceptable—his nightmares were crowded enough.

He shuddered. He had tried to avoid his haunting dreams by not sleeping, but all that did was turn him into a zombie, a specter rivaling those in his night-mares. He soon realized there was no escape from his mind, just as there was no escape from the long arm of Maelstrom. The corpse-filled dream that followed him was now a part of him, always eager and ready to rise in its dogged pursuit.

A familiar chill skipped across Greer's scalp and he shivered, knowing a legion of corpses was waiting for him now, summoned by his thoughts. He closed his eyes and sank into his living hell.

Filling his mind is a field of whispering corpses ris-ing from the ground. He can't hear what they say, but knows instinctively this is critical some how. They sit up in their graves, staring at him, blank-eyed, with dirt in their mouths. He pulls back, horrified, choking. The skin across his back bunches and puckers in a prickly wave.

He is terrified of having dirt in his mouth.

The corpses drift as if in water, floating, sucking him in. Slow as molasses, he moves among them. He knows them all well; this vision is a guided tour of his life's work.

His garden.

The corpses stare at him and smile, knowing some-thing he doesn't. He wants to leave, but he can't stop now.

He is in too deep. He doesn't want to know any more and turns to leave. But a lone figure from the back motions to him, drawing him closer.

His heart fills with dread as he tries to see the face on the last corpse. He can't make it out, even though something seems terribly familiar. This frightens him even more, and panic trips through his intestines. Still, he must know—

Who is the last corpse in his garden?

Like a fool, he continues, the wanting and the not wanting writhing inside him like a pit of vipers. He goes deeper and deeper into the garden, past the faces of those he has killed. Yet what he pursues seems even farther away—

Greer jerked in his chair, breaking free of the scene with a shudder. He gripped his desk with rigid hands while his back sprouted a scalding river of sweat. He panted, looking down at his desk, to the new file with the runway photo of his missing blonde.

He must find her—alive.

His fingers drummed against the desktop. This was now a Level Two situation. If events escalated to Level Three, he was authorized to get involved. With idiots like Bennett screwing up, he might have to get involved just to run damage control.

"Where are you, little girl?" he whispered. He had to make sure she was not destined for his garden.

•

"Whew," Mady said, sliding down in her seat on their fourth bus. "Thank goodness there is precious little on these night buses."

"How accurate, for I am certain little of what I've seen tonight is … precious," Carter chimed.

Mady couldn't help chuckling at Carter's assessment. In their ride about London, they shared their second bus with a couple of young kids wearing wild make-up and mysterious costumes. The following bus held a single occupant, a fierce old woman who glared at them for the entire ride until they exited.

Finally they were alone.

"God, I'm tired," she said, hunching her shoulders, "We can't keep running like this." In her hands she fidgeted with Carter's bloody handkerchief. She held it out to him with a sheepish look. "I don't suppose you still want this."

He spread the cloth against his leg and traced where her blood marred the snowy whiteness. He sat still and silent for so long she finally glanced at him.

What is he holding back?

"Where did you leave it?" he asked harshly. His voice grated as he smoothed out the ruined cloth.

"I stuffed it into a seat on our second bus," she said.

Abruptly he turned on her and she drew back, alarmed by the intensity of his expression.

"We can't let them touch you like this again," he declared.

He grabbed her by both arms and shook her until her head wobbled. "What you did back at the restaurant was wild and daring—and insanely foolish. You must promise me you won't do anything like that again."

Mady wanted to proclaim her right to vengeance. She was proud of everything she'd accomplished in the last several hours, but the concern in Carter's eyes was heart stopping. "What are you not telling me?" she asked.

He let go of her and sat back in his seat. "So many

have been touched by the coin. I couldn't bear to see you hurt, or worse."

"Carter, I'm a third degree black belt in Kenpo karate. I can handle myself. It was martial arts that eventually brought me to the study of ancient cultures. In the dojo I learned the philosophy of 'no right, no wrong, only different.' The past, you see, holds no agenda, it is simply evidence of what was different."

In deprecating tones, she clarified. "At least that's what I used to think." She shrugged and waved off his concern. "The coin's presence has managed to prove that entire philosophy wrong. Anyhow," she added with sparkling eyes, "I've been on some pretty remote and primitive dig sites, not to mention the dressing room at a photo shoot."

She moved her hands, executing a simple movement with deadly grace. Commanding the power of life and death still gave her a thrill. "A girl's got to limit her vulnerability," she finished.

"But," Carter argued, "your martial arts training didn't help you when they put in the chip."

"Yes, and I assure you one ass-kicking hasn't balanced the books." She stared out the window, noticing the lightening sky. For all her bravado, she was dead tired and running blind. "I do agree that whoever is after us—after the coins, is beyond anything I can handle. But you can't protect me, either."

She gave him a hard look and jutted her chin at him, challenging him to take the lead. "So, you tell me—what do we do?"

His fingers tapped on the bloody cloth while he took his time to answer. Mady pulled her knees up and propped them on the back of the seat in front of her, waiting. Her long legs were angled, bringing her body up next to his. He was so stable and so cool-headed—she didn't want to think about confronting tonight's events without his help.

"What I suggest," he said finally, his voice low, "is that we should be afraid—very afraid. If your theory is proven correct, it will bring down all the known truths. Everything we believe about our species, our planet, our God—everything will change."

He ran one hand through his hair and his voice shook. It was the first real crack in his calm demeanor she had seen all night. She reared back to look at him. His face was wracked with conflict.

"Finding out the truth after all this time," he said. "Learning our origins are different than anyone imagined will rip through the fiber of modern society with devastating impact. A cataclysmic shift must certainly come with this change you are so vehement about. I'm not so sure everyone's ready for a truth this big, Madelyn."

She stared at the silent suggestion in his eyes, appalled.

He talks like it's a death sentence.

"You're not saying we should bury it, are you?" She moved to sit up, ready to refute his suggestion.

"No, no, of course not," he said, pulling her back to the seat. "But I think we should learn what it's about before we get ourselves killed."

"You're not telling me something—"

"Just translate—"

"There's nothing to translate," she protested. "I have no message, no confirmed sample like the Rosetta Stone to—" She stopped mid-sentence, halted by the intensity of his look.

"There must be a message of some kind," he said. "Look again—you'll find something, I know it."

She stalled, uncertain.

He's right. All the answers are in the symbols.

"We work on you deciphering the symbols," he said, wrapping his arm around her shoulders again, "—and we tell no one. I think that has kept us alive so far."

She pulled his arm closer and pressed into the seat. "Thank God you intercepted me tonight. I'm lucky to be alive—to have escaped that thing and what it was doing in my body." She jerked with a sudden shudder and he squeezed her shoulder in silent support. "As for who else wants the coins," she whispered, "and the potential they possess? You're right, that could be—"

"Anyone," he answered, shaking his head no. "And since we don't know who they are, telling no one is definitely the safest approach."

"You think telling no one—" she repeated, not quite convinced.

"Is much better—" He nodded like a bobble-head doll, making her laugh.

"So, the answer—" she prodded.

"The answer," he responded, his face lighting up, "is for you to solve the mystery of the symbols, as you were meant to."

The look of blind faith in his eyes was compelling. He was counting on her do this. She stared at her clenched hands and willed them to relax. The passion for understanding the coins and their symbols shot past her exhaustion, fueled in part by her reluctance to disappoint Carter.

She flexed her fingers. "To do that, I need my notes

from my hotel room."

•

St. Germain stared at the lonely abandoned street. Since the police left with the injured, ugly man from the restaurant it had been so quiet, his hope was flagging.

"Can you see him?" Henri asked.

St. Germain looked up, astonished to see a second Renault come swiftly down the street. At the intersection before the eatery, it came to a sudden stop, then jetted through the light and parked behind the first Renault.

They watched as a big man got out and walked to the first car. He got in and reached below the seat. When he sat up, the car fired up and he drove away.

"So, a clean-up crew," Solomon said. "The big man will stash the first car and then return to his vehicle."

The laptop showed a repeating pattern in the path of the chip. "If Mr. Carter and his lady are being tracked by the chip, it may be the people in charge have discovered the chip has been discarded. Perhaps that is what has spurred all this activity."

He paused again, one finger tapping his chin.

Things were happening so fast.

He groaned and rubbed his face, squeezing the bridge of his nose. He must get closer; all he had to go on was intuition. He hoped it was enough, for he was taking a huge risk. "Henri, we don't have a lot of time. You have much to do."

•

Twenty minutes later, Henri returned to the Rolls, ready for Carter and the woman to come back. Before getting back in, he noticed the early lightening sky. Soon they would need to move. While the big limo belonged to the night, in the daylight they would be too conspicuous to maintain this surveillance.

Looking over his shoulder, he saw his cousin resting, his eyes closed. It had been a long night and they were still a long way from home. He asked softly, knowing St. Germain was not asleep. "Where are they? Are you still getting a location from the chip?"

"The chip is still broadcasting, but it is traveling in a circle. My esteem of our wayward pair escalates," Solomon said, sitting up. "For this reason among others, I would very much like to know what connects them to our cause."

He looked at the sky—dawn was upon them. "When they come for their car, be ready to get right behind them. We must be in a position to render immediate assistance."

•

5:30 AM
Soho

The last bus left them off where they began. Carter and Mady, exhausted, crawled back into the Jag. He drove, grateful for the short distance to her hotel. *Just get the notes from her room*, he thought, *and she'll discover something she's missed.* He looked over at her. She was alive, riding her second wind.

"Cripes," she cried out. She held her left fist to her forehead and looked ready to weep. The other hand she waved in the air, writing on an imaginary board.

"This is ridiculous—I have nothing to work with— just these symbols in a circle. If our lives depend on me deciphering something out of what we have, then I hope you own a spare black suit."

He was sympathetic to her agony. He could only imagine how difficult it must be—so close, and yet so far. "There's something there, I just know it. We can't give up," he said, smiling with all the encouragement he could muster.

She gave him a slanted look while not deigning to respond, before returning to her wild mutterings. When she brought her hand back up to draw in the air, he knew she was in another world.

They were within sight of her hotel when the Jaguar sputtered and lurched, threatening to stall. Carter instantly pulled into an adjacent empty lot just as the car died. He stared askance at the Jaguar dash, unable to comprehend why his vehicle should act so.

Their destination was about one hundred yards away. He groaned and looked at Mady. She still had her eyes closed. Lost in the symbols, she hadn't noticed they were stopped. The early morning light highlighted the purple shadows beneath her eyes. He hated to tell her they had to walk. Fire-breathing dragon or not, she was as tired as he was. He got out and walked to her door, opening it.

The cool morning air kissed her face and she opened her eyes, turning her head to see where they were. Just then, a great Rolls-Royce limousine pulled up into the lot beside them. Through a lowered window they heard a cultured male voice call out. "May I be of any assistance?"

It took a heartbeat for Carter to make eye contact with Mady. As one, they turned to stare at the distinguished looking gentleman who watched them from the limousine.

Carter's thoughts scrambled. *Is this a threat, or an-*

other piece in the puzzle? He scrutinized the man from the limo. In his forties, he had a dark complexion with a Mediterranean look.

Carter didn't move. Somehow he couldn't reconcile himself to seeing this man in league with the man from the restaurant. But then, Sir Roger was a distinguished-looking fellow as well.

Carter wanted to be suspicious, but it didn't seem right. If a man like this paid to have surveillance done, he waited at home for the reports. He didn't cruise around getting in the way and making contact.

All of Carter's instincts told him this was not their adversary. However, while the man's sudden appearance didn't feel threatening, Carter knew there was still something afoot. He looked at his Jaguar and knew they had tampered with it to orchestrate this little tête-à-tête.

If he is not an adversary, then what is he?

Something about the Rolls-Royce was familiar. Before he could decide how, the man spoke again and the hair on Carter's neck rose up.

"You are being followed by some very nasty people, Mr. Carter. Do you know why?"

"Who are you, sir?" Carter asked in return.

The man climbed out of the Rolls and offered his hand. "I am Solomon St. Germain. The fellow driving is my cousin, Henri."

Carter looked at Mady, his heart now tripping at a mighty clip. He was ready to grab her and run for their lives, but she was studying the two men with no sense of alarm.

He hesitated, suddenly unsure in the face of her acquiescence. While he wanted to know what this man knew, his insides were telling him to run. He watched Mady continue with her inspection, remaining cool and interested. Carter fought the urge to gnash his teeth and focused instead on her intent expression. When she displayed no alarm, he swallowed his fear.

"Mr. St. Germain, we would be most grateful to hear what you know." He reached out to grasp the gentleman's extended hand.

At this point, Madelyn stretched her legs out the door. Carter took her hand as she rose. "Mr. St. Germain, I am Madelyn Fox. How did you know Carter's name, and how is it that you knew we were being followed?" She followed Carter's lead and offered St. Germain her hand.

He took her hand with a light touch and a look of admiration. "Miss Fox, I commend you for your recent tactics. Thank God there are women like you in this world," he said, eyes twinkling. "I am aware of your situation because I, too, was following you."

Mady jerked her hand back with startling quickness and stepped in front of Carter, who stiffened with alarm. "That's why this car looks familiar," he said. "I saw you circling the hotel from Mady's window."

St. Germain held up his hands in innocent protest. "Please, I understand your reservations." He gave each a direct look with his clear eyes. "If you'll let me explain, you'll see I am no threat to you. May I suggest we retire to the limousine so we can discuss 'our' situation—in safety? You may keep the door open if you like. We will remain here, in clear view."

He swept his arm out, indicating the busy street. "I promise you, I mean no harm. I am here because I believe we may be able to help each other."

Carter passed a fleeting glance at Mady. She flicked her eyebrows in return, displaying only curiosity. "All right, Mr. St. Germain," Carter said.

St. Germain climbed back into the Rolls, leaving them room to sit by the open door. They climbed in and he waited until they were settled.

Mady sank into the soft leather seat. A look of relief spread across her face, and she exhaled, "Ohhhh."

Carter gave the inside of the luxurious automobile a discreet yet appreciative glance before asking, "How did you come to be following us?"

St. Germain answered immediately. "I was following the electronic transmission of a tracking device," he said. "One that was, I assume, implanted on one of you." He pointed to his laptop on the fold-down table. "My guess is you left it behind on one of your bus rides."

Carter and Mady sat up in the seat to better view the computer screen. They watched a circular path displayed on a map of greater London. "How is it you possess information on this device?" Mady asked.

St. Germain sat back and frowned, his expression turning dark. "Miss Fox, I am aware of it," he said, reaching into his pocket, "because one of these devices was removed from the body of a murdered relative. I am here because I intend to find the entity responsible for this, and see that they are stopped."

Carter took the plastic bag St. Germain offered. He instantly recognized the small object it held. He passed the bag to Mady. She glanced at it, lips pinched, before handing it back to St. Germain.

Silent tension pulsed in the back seat while the sound of London's morning streets wavered in the background. Carter thrummed his fingers on the leather armrest. Mady gazed out the open door, wordless.

"All right, all right," Mady muttered under her breath.

Carter heard and knew she was "conversing" with her intuitive voice. He was relieved to see she felt St. Germain wasn't a threat, yet he was concerned about what she was about to do.

St. Germain tilted his head in Mady's direction. She looked him in the eye for a span of several seconds before saying, "The chip is a common link, Mr. St. Germain. But that does not solve the mystery. Why are these devices being used on us? What else do we have in common?"

Carter lurched forward in shock. He caught her eye and shook his head.

She returned his look, her foot tapping an agitated beat against the leather seat. Her eyes glowed with a fire of certainty and conviction that Carter didn't share. He swallowed hard and shook his head again.

She leaned toward him, and stated emphatically, "Yes."

Tension spread like spilled ink. Carter turned toward the open door and set one foot on the ground, desperately wanting to run. He watched the passing traffic—so remote and uninvolved—so safe—he wanted to shout with the unfairness of it. Sweat trickled out of his hair and ran down his cheekbone; he swiped at it absently. He was afraid—afraid enough for all of them—and it paralyzed him.

A quick look at Mady told him she was certain, for her brilliant blue eyes shone like she understood everything she needed to know. He sighed in amazement. After all she'd been through tonight, how could she still be so sure of herself?

It must be her spirit, that goddess power, he thought with a tentative smile. In his pocket he caressed his Egyptian coin. The gold warmed immediately and he wondered, as he always did—*how does it do that?* He cleared his throat. Coaxing his vocal chords to produce sound was like moving busted concrete. "If you are so certain—"

"As certain as you were earlier," she replied.

He remembered the moment when he knew her body held a tracking device. He sat back in his seat and tried to relax, while keeping his one foot out the door. His ears hummed and he shook his head. He knew what was coming. His knees quivered just thinking about it.

I can't hide the coin any more.

He groaned, and nodded yes.

Mady gave him a quick smile of encouragement before turning to St. Germain. "Is it possible we have … this … in common?" She turned back to Carter and they locked eyes.

Carter saw the fearless conviction in her eyes and knew he could not fight her. By habit, he chose to pull out his fake coin. With a smooth flip, his nimble fingers began the dance. The gold glittered in the early morning light, claiming every eye.

Seconds passed before St. Germain reacted. He gasped and put his hand to his throat, staring at the golden piece. His speechless mouth hung open and his eyes locked on the coin.

As St. Germain's reaction became more profound, Carter's excitement mounted. He shot a quick glance at Mady and her eyes said, *I told you so.*

"See. I was right," she mouthed.

Carter's heart went faster and his palms broke a sweat, making the coin slippery. He fumbled, then tried to catch it, but sent the gold sailing into the air instead. For one precipitous instant, the coin hung suspended, daring them all to look. It gracefully turned and twisted, flashing end over end—until St. Germain neatly plucked it from the air.

He stared at the coin as if it were still molten. Trembling fingers held it to the morning light. Breathless, he stammered, "Dear … Lord in heaven, you have—"

•

Jack Greer slumped into his chair and thought about banging his head on the desk.

What in the hell is going on with this assignment?

He sagged with disbelief. The double-edged sword of accountability hung above his miserable neck, and he could hear it slice through the air, coming ominously close. Not only was he missing one very expensive piece of hardware and one agent, but a second agent now joined the list of missing.

He hit re-dial for Mason Andrews. Still no answer. Greer decided it was Andrews' head that he needed to beat against the desk.

The girl was loose, the chip was gone, Bennett was in jail, and Andrews was missing. Greer thrummed his fingers against the desk. He now had a Level Three situation. He picked up the photograph and the familiar twinge of guilt went for his gut.

What grief did I bring into your life?

"Careful little girl," he growled, dragging his hand through his hair. "You might think you're pretty smart right about now—but I have to call The One. And the topic of our discussion is going to be—you."

He groaned and dropped his head into his hands. *This night*, he thought, *just keeps getting worse and worse.* He sat back and rolled his head from side to side. Placing his hands on his chin and forehead, he gave a sharp tug.

His neck popped like a string of bursting balloons.

"Ohhh, yeah," he gasped. He turned his attention to the special phone on his desk with a secure landline. All Level Three assignments obligated Greer to make a phone report to Maelstrom. He picked up the runway photo. She really was beautiful. It was a shame he had entered her life.

Stay focused and get control of this situation.

Before he called Maelstrom, he had one more option. He threw the photograph down on his desk and picked up his cell phone. "Mason 'ol buddy, I hope you're still alive, because I'm going to need you."

•

The only thing wounded on Mason Andrews was his pride.

When he came to, the first thing he noticed was the cell phone vibrating in his pants pocket. Then he smelled the duct tape plastered across his mouth. Opening one eye, he realized his face was shoved against the Renault's dusty floor mats.

Uh oh. Greer won't like this.

Mason mentally reviewed the coming confrontation with Greer. "So, Jack, this little Frenchie guy—" He shook his head and cringed, then thought again. "Jack, there were three of them—"

That was better. He would lie.

It was because of the girl. I know the girl.

"So, Jack," he rehearsed, mumbling his excuse

through the duct tape across his mouth. "That's how they got the jump on me. You see—I was star-gazing at the pretty girl, trying to figure out, how do I know her?"

Yeah right, he thought. *That ought to get me slapped up the side of my head.*

He wiggled to test his bindings and ground his teeth with frustration. He was covered with a blanket so no one could see him. He squirmed until his feet touched the door, then he started kicking. Sooner or later someone would pass and hear him.

Suddenly the door opened. *Thank God,* he thought. Beneath the tape, he attempted to compose his features into that of a bewildered victim. Then the blanket lifted away and he stared up into the hot glaring face of Jack Greer.

"Stop that racket, you fool," Greer snarled. He grabbed the end of the duct tape and gave a vicious yank.

"Ooooww," Mason cried, cringing as the tape ripped from his face.

"One word," Greer threatened with a withering stink-eye. "One word and I will reassign you Stateside. You're lucky I need you, so get out and shut up."

Greer pulled out a small razor knife and slashed the tape wrapping Mason's hands. He watched with a hard look bereft of any sympathy or understanding as Mason removed his other bindings and crawled clumsily out from the rear floorboards, dusting off his hands and his clothes. He rubbed at the skin around his mouth, picking little chunks of adhesive from his whiskers.

"The girl has to be found," Greer hissed. "She dumped her chip. We're going back to the office. If she used a credit card to pay for anything then we'll catch her—if it isn't too late."

Growling, he reached out and slapped Andrews against the side of his head. "You better pray we find her."

CHAPTER SIX

6:00 AM
London

St. Germain gasped with astonishment. "You have a coin!"

He held the gold piece to the light in a grip of death. The blood pumping in his head drowned out his own words from his ears, so hard did his pulse pound. His hand trembled and he closed his fingers around the coin as his reality slipped into the unknown.

In all the countless generations his family guarded the ancient secret, never was there any mention of another coin. He stared at the gold. The sacred symbols winked at him in the early morning foggy light.

What do the symbols mean?

He struggled to collect himself. He didn't dare look at Carter or the young woman for fear of what his face would reveal. Events were cascading toward the unimaginable. In his chest his heart banged around like a loose cannon. A single bead of cold sweat trickled down his back as he realized—

I will have to tell them.

Mady grabbed his wrist with a strength and quickness that startled him. He looked to the front, to Henri, whose eyes watched them through the rear view mirror. He nodded subtly, setting his cousin at ease. These people were not a threat, but what they knew and how they were involved was something Solomon had to find out.

Mady held him with a fearless grip. When he leaned back, she responded, coming forward to maintain her hold on him. He thought of the injured man from the restaurant and he understood her perfectly—she was capable of doing what was necessary.

How these new events impacted Solomon's family brought him a wave of sick anticipation. Long seconds passed while he waited ... waited to hear her say the words he sought for so long.

She gave him the full intensity of her gaze. Her voice rang clear as she challenged him. "You have one, too, don't you?"

St. Germain snatched his hand back, rubbing at his wrist. While these were not the words he wanted to hear, his hope was not to be defeated. He still held Carter's coin. His mind spun out of control while his fingers rubbed the coin, caressing it, feeling its solid form.

Suddenly he froze, and looked askance at the piece, questioning what his senses were telling him. Surprised, he looked up.

I do not have time for such games.

He slammed the coin down next to the laptop. With a grim set to his mouth, he reached for the console where he kept a gun.

"Wait, please," Mady whispered.

She was very beautiful and Solomon didn't want to

believe her capable of duplicity. He stopped. Still, he kept his hand on the console as she unzipped a small pocket of her jeans. He glared at her with indignation, daring her to try something.

She removed a small black bag. A gold coin slipped out to grace her palm. Solomon's world tilted. He knew—

Nothing in my life will ever be the same.

He didn't know whether to be thrilled or terrified.

"Please, take it," she said. "It's authentic, I promise."

His relief was instantaneous as he took the coin. He hefted it and felt the heavy center. On one side, the mysterious symbols maintained their impenetrable circle. He didn't know whether to laugh or cry, and considered both actions worthy—for he never expected to see such a thing happen in his lifetime. He closed his hand around the gold piece and prayed.

Please, give me answers.

His mind ran through the impossible territory he was considering, his emotions fully at war. To be a Keeper of the ancient secret was a lifetime commitment. By necessity, countless sacrifices were called for in the interest of security—sacrifices he made with pride. When he took the oath, he assumed a somewhat ascetic lifestyle, giving up his personal life for the sake of protecting the secret and the sacred writing.

Yet, although he gave willingly, he never knew what the writing said. Just as every Keeper before him, he would do anything to know what the symbols meant. But now, more than ever, if he was going to protect his family and the ancient secret in a world grown too small, he had to know.

Dare I wonder—is this worth all we have sacrificed?

He sighed, the sound deep, and to his ears, tainted with weariness. The weight of life and death decisions filled his voice as he asked, "Will you allow me to look into your eyes?"

The woman nodded, sensing what he wanted. She reached out and gave him her hand and leaned forward, this time giving instead of demanding. Her touch was warm, the skin smooth and dry. He felt the pulse at her wrist beat easy and steady.

Her face was beautiful, matching her eyes. They were a pale Nordic blue accented with dark blue lights. Without hesitation she locked her gaze with his ... and let him in. He looked long and deep with no surprises. Over the years he had searched many in this fashion, and this woman's eyes were clear to their depths.

A glance at Carter showed that one sat ramrod straight in the seat, his expression open, yet filled with challenge. Undoubtedly, Carter would not have his integrity questioned, regardless of the circumstances.

St. Germain sighed. It seemed events were forcing them together. He must trust them, for time was running short. He set her coin on the table with the symbols facing up.

"You never answered me, Mr. St. Germain," she demanded. She glanced quickly at Carter, a look of triumph on her face.

St. Germain hesitated. Old habits die slowly. He turned to stare out the window, frowning.

This responsibility was not meant to rest with one person.

He felt Mady's intense gaze upon him. Her foot fluttered to life as she waited his response. Silence passed and the tension returned to the Rolls-Royce.

Still he held his answer.

Carter shifted in his seat and glanced between the two of them. His voice was dry after his long silence. "I for one, need to see this nightmare finished, or I may never sleep again. If we want to be free, we have to work together."

He reached into his other pocket and withdrew something—another gold coin. It glittered in the pale morning light with a sentient energy before Carter sent it tumbling across his knuckles, drawing all eyes.

"Apparently," Carter said, "the three of us have lived with a knowledge that has demanded a high price, measured by the lives of loved ones."

Carefully, he continued, speaking remotely, his eyes drawn with theirs to the tumbling coin. "The coin and its symbols have altered our lives with its infinite implications, even without us knowing what the symbols mean." The coin glittered in his hand, challenging all of them.

"Everything," he offered, "comes back to the symbols and their reason for being here—and tonight's events indicate there does seem to be a ... purpose."

"Who left them?" Carter asked. He looked to St. Germain, who remained rigid in his seat since the appearance of the second coin. Solomon's eyes followed the magical path of Carter's tumbling coin, slowly shaking his head no.

Carter went on, his voice smooth and his clipped British accent purred, as hypnotic as the dance of the coin. "What are they trying to tell us? More important for the moment, who else wants what we have?" His questions lingered in the air, begging for answers while the coin continued to whisk through his fingers.

St. Germain stared, still shaking his head in disbelief. He glanced to the front, needing to affirm his cousin's presence in a world gone mad. When Carter produced a second coin, Solomon physically had to hold back a shout of hysterical laughter.

His family had kept such a coin secret for thousands of years. Now, in the space of minutes, two more were revealed to him. His mind rocketed, even as he was rendered motionless.

Now what?

Carter captured his tumbling coin and placed it on the table, symbols up, next to the other two. "Besides the duplicate, we have two coins, one Egyptian, one Sumerian," he said, lining them up side-by-side.

St. Germain never could have imagined this night. He traced the ancient writing with his finger, passing from coin to coin. "I see cuneiform," he said, "your Sumerian coin?" He looked to Mady and she nodded yes.

His fingers traced the exotic impressions on Carter's Egyptian coin. "And then hieroglyphs." The coins lined up like soldiers, shoulder to shoulder, battle-ready after passing so many millennia in silence.

Mady picked up the fake coin and handed it back to Carter, leaving the two authentic coins side by side.

"*You are the Children of Gods,*" she read. "From Sumeria, about 3100 BCE." She pushed the Sumerian coin toward St. Germain.

"From the time of the great pyramid, about 2450 BCE, we have, *Find Your Power in the Greatest Temple.*"

She looked straight at him, her beautiful eyes pleading, and his heart broke for her, for he knew what she was going to ask.

"Do you know what these statements mean?"

There was so much he couldn't tell her, but the truth was, he didn't know. He shook his head. Disappointment briefly crushed the hope in her eyes.

She pulled a face of despair, but pressed on, determined. "What language is on your coin? I assume there is a second language with some message on it, as with ours?"

"Yes," he answered. He blinked and gave the smallest nod. "There is Hebrew."

She leaned toward him, the excitement alive in her eyes. "Are the symbols just in a circle, or is there more?"

Mouth suddenly dry, he stared back, trying to moisten his lips. His heart hammered, matching the ringing in his ears.

"You see," she said in a rush, "if I had more, something beyond the simple circle, a message—" She shrugged, clearly desperate.

St. Germain would have laughed … and probably could have foamed at the mouth as well, but he couldn't breathe. He watched her lips move, hoping she was at last going to say the words he had prayed for all his life.

"Somewhere," she continued, "there is a message."

She paused, and in that moment, Solomon searched his body for his abandoned breath. Hysterics hovered near by, ready for an opening to rush in. He held the panic at bay, focusing on her mouth as she at last, formed the words that would change his life.

"There has to be a message somewhere," she said. "I don't believe they would leave this many clues for no reason. If I could just get my hands on a real length of text, I know I could translate it. You see, I think the circle is their alphabet. They have twenty-five symbols to our twenty-six, because none of them—" Abruptly she stopped, her brows laced in concern. "Mr. St. Germain, are you all right?" she asked.

Too late, too late, Solomon thought. His breath was gone and forgotten, eclipsed by the ancient, royal command his family followed for over three thousand years—

Reveal only to those who know the meaning of the symbols.

Perhaps she is the one, he thought.

Solomon realized his need for air, and hauled in a great breath. Seeking the assurance of Henri's steady brown gaze in the rearview mirror with a quick glance, he spoke around his thundering heart, voicing words he never thought he'd say.

"Yes, I have such a coin as these. The symbols are not in a circle. They are in a block of writing. Perhaps you are right—what I have could be the message you seek. Would you like to examine my coin?"

She looked at Carter. He stared out the open door, appearing unconcerned, as though they discussed where to have lunch.

"Yes, I would," she answered, slumping back into her seat. "And I hope it's close by. I've already had one long, heck of a night."

"Henri, we are going home," Solomon said.

"*Oui.* Immediately."

•

St. Germain Townhouse, London

Mady ached with exhaustion, and the comfort of the big limo was numbing. She wanted to see this new coin and then sleep for a week. When she woke up, there would be a new world. She rolled her shoulders and looked at Carter, who sat quiet after his earlier impassioned speech. Thankfully, it didn't take them long to reach the St. Germain townhouse.

When they parked, she watched as Henri checked their perimeter before opening the doors; from the Rolls they moved quickly into the lift. Henri's heightened sense of awareness was contagious, and she peeled her eyes around the garage.

They huddled together in the elevator, and as the doors closed, a communal sigh of relief filled the enclosure. Silently, they traveled to the top floor and the main entrance.

Mady entered and glanced around. The opulent decor was elegant, tasteful ... and filled with treasure. She walked past the threshold and stopped to stare, her eyes startled. Before her were enough objects d'art to fill an entire showroom at the Metropolitan. She saw Egyptian and Byzantine art decorated the entryway and beyond into the first reception room.

Her mouth fell open in awe. Her fingers twitched. She glanced at Carter. He stood near the door, engrossed in the contents of a massive wall mounted teak case. Within it was a section of stone relief depicting a chariot and driver with a royal archer hunting a great cat. Etched in stunning detail, she could count the snarling cat's whiskers.

She moved to join Carter in his inspection when her eye caught a series of papyrus scrolls in a hermetically sealed case. She began reading. When she realized it told the myth of the great flood, her mouth fell open again ... and she was lost.

"My family," St. Germain said, "has accumulated considerable archaeological wealth over the years. Most of what you see here has never been outside a St. Germain home."

He passed by them and went to a side door, waiting for them to follow. Mady heard him clear his throat several times before she forced herself away from the papyrus. When she passed by Carter, she grabbed his hand, pulling him along.

St. Germain was patient. When they gave him their attention, he swept his arm out in invitation. They preceded him into the next room for several steps until gradually, they came to another halt.

"Oh ... my ... heavens," Mady whispered. She swept her eyes around the unclassified artifacts and was torn in a hundred directions. She moved left and spied a display case filled with tablets written in cuneiform and dipped in gold, dated 3400 BCE according to the tag.

"Ohhh," she breathed when she saw gold Egyptian funerary masks next to Celtic jewelry. By the time she noticed the marble throne carved with Greek gods and beasts, she gave up trying to make intelligent sounds.

She shot a quick glance at Carter. He was still at the threshold. Entranced, he stared in wonder with his mouth unattractively agape.

Thus reminded, Mady shut her own slack-jawed mouth. "I cannot believe—" she said, craning her neck to look all around the room. "There is so much." She shook her head in denial. "Never would I think it possible for such a private collection to exist."

She turned back to Carter, but he remained oblivious. He stood in the center of the room, turning in a circle, taking one tiny step at a time. If she weren't so tired, she'd laugh.

The clink of china brought her focus to Henri as he

entered with a massive tea service. She sniffed the distinctive smell of bergamot and her mouth watered.

"Earl Grey, *mademoiselle*." Henri poured the tea, and the bergamot finally caught Carter's British nose. She grinned at his antics as he came to sit next to her.

"Did you see—?" he whispered. He made big eyes of astonishment at her while he accepted a cup from Henri. Speechless, his words trailed off and he gave up as he sipped the hot beverage.

After serving them, Henri took his own cup and retired to the window where he perched on a stool, watching the street below. *Thank God,* Mady thought. At least someone is thinking security while she wallowed from excitement to rage, then on to exhaustion before stuttering from a new thrill.

She held the hot cup in her chilled hands, feeling the fatigue of the long night grind in her muscles. She gave Carter the once-over, and said, "I don't know how you do it."

He blew on his tea and feigned innocence at her perusal. "Do what, darling?" he asked.

"Look dapper," she said. "How in the hell do you manage to appear so fresh? And don't tell me it's your British genes, because I have them also … and mine are falling down on the job, royally." She rubbed at her face, pressing her tired eyes. "I feel like a road kill," she moaned.

Carter wrinkled his nose, making a show of delicately sniffing the wind. She swung her toe at his shin, just missing him.

Relaxed for the first time in hours, she enjoyed the brief respite. She sipped her tea and brought her mind back to the task of translating the alien symbols. Her heart began to pick up its pace as she went through the familiar possibilities.

St. Germain returned. He took the time to carefully prepare his tea. She watched him take a cautious sip of the hot liquid. When he inhaled deeply of the fragrant blend, she squirmed.

He's stalling.

Finally, he exhaled a long and lonely sigh. She tilted her head at the pain-filled sound; it echoed with the agony of a difficult, long-fought battle.

He sat up and put his cup down. Without preamble, he reached into his jacket pocket and pulled out a coin.

Mady choked, her breath caught in her throat with the tea. Adrenaline rocketed through her and she lurched forward to set her cup down, splashing the tea on her hands. "Dammit," she mumbled. She fretted with wiping her fingers on the serviette, oblivious of the men watching her.

Her only focus was the new coin. She silently begged the gods to please, please give her something to work with. The room receded into the background as she stared at the gold piece. It glittered, daring her mind, teasing her theory, torturing her with its presence. She heard Carter rise and felt his warmth when he came to stand behind her. He bent down over the back of her chair, putting his chin at her shoulder.

They stared at the third coin.

She hefted it for weight and grinned, slanting a sideways glance at him. "It's real."

He grunted and one eyebrow jerked, indignant.

"Look," she whispered, pointing, "random duplication." With a hushed reverence, she traced the marks with a trembling finger. A shiver soared through her like a hissing kettle, and she closed her eyes. "Carter, this script has repeating characters." She looked at St. Germain and tried to talk with her major organs crowded into her throat. "I think there's a message here."

She turned back to the coins. Without looking up, she thrust her hand out. She cleared her throat and demanded, "Glass—"

Within seconds one appeared in her opened palm.

She studied the coin with the sharp magnification. "Not just repeating characters—" she called out, "but something else. There are marks here that we don't see in the alphabet circles. Carter—your coin."

Snapping her fingers, she held out her hand until she felt his coin pressed into her palm. She placed it next to the Hebrew coin and studied the two with the magnifying glass, back and forth, again and again.

She stood up and dug in her front pocket, her eyes on the floor. She dared not look at Carter or St. Germain until she was certain. Pulling out the velvet bag, she fumbled with the tie. She forced herself to pause, breathing through pursed lips, flexing and wiggling her fingers until her heart slowed down.

The tie came loose and the coin slipped out. She placed the three coins side by side and brought them into sharp focus with a sweep of her hand.

"On the Hebrew coin I see small marks—nuances in the impressions. They look like nicks, but considering the pristine condition of the coin, I rather doubt it. My guess is they could be punctuation."

Excitement filled her chest, ready to explode. She went back to the coins and raised her hand, snapping her fingers again, calling, "Pen and paper."

This appeared while her hand was still in mid-air.

She made a series of counts and calculations, her foot tapping madly all the while. For several seconds she continued, mumbling and scratching at the paper. She looked at what she had and cautiously withheld any reaction. She ran her calculations again, and got the same results. When she got the same results for the third time, she stopped and stared at her scribbling. A smile began, slowly—and she looked at her writing again. When she knew for sure, she closed her eyes, savoring the incredible discovery.

I did it.

"I have it," she said. She put the glass down and raised her eyes to Carter. She grinned like a fool, she knew, but she couldn't stop herself—she was about to bust.

"I have it—no … I mean—you have it. Your coin is a Rosetta coin. Look," she said, holding up the Hebrew coin. "This block of alien symbols is the other three messages—cuneiform, hieroglyphs, and Hebrew, all duplicated in the alien script—just like the Rosetta stone. This gives us enough for a translation.

"They were brilliant," she whispered. "They put the same messages in four languages, spread across three coins. You had to have all three coins together for comparison to see it." She captured the men with her gaze. "Whoever left these coins did so with a plan. In fact," she said, waving the Rosetta coin. "This coin is, in its design, very similar to the actual Rosetta stone. I have to consider they are deliberately so. At any rate, this clue promises more, I'm sure." She turned to Carter, her voice quivering with passion.

"Think of the places of discovery, Carter—Jerusalem, Sumer, Egypt—all played a part in what they wanted us to know.

"First, we have two dynamic civilizations that sprang up suddenly out of nowhere … cultures that exhibited remarkable levels of unprecedented velocity in their development. In the midst of these cultures, this ancient race left evidence of their presence—coins bearing the messages that link them all together. If we search the artifacts of other great civilizations, there are more of these coins—I know it.

"They wanted us to find them," she continued, seeing Henri come to join their circle. "Oh, they wanted us to find them, but not too soon. They knew the knowledge they were leaving behind had the potential to disrupt our society. So they scattered the clues across history, leaving them at key points for time to deliver when it was right … thousands of years later, in a future where we are hopefully sophisticated enough to understand."

She watched St. Germain and Carter to see if they were following her. Carter had the great "ah-ha" expression, while St. Germain's face looked like a battlefield.

Someone else with a secret.

Still, St. Germain made no move to stop her. Whatever he knew, she hadn't contradicted it yet. "The premise for leaving clues with a specific message is to attract the right attention. Qualify your clue delivery, and you automatically qualify your hunter." She paused to get her breath, and gulped her tea.

Carter nodded, encouraging. "Tell us more, Mady."

"They left clues," she said, "geared toward those uniquely qualified in the sciences who needed to understand the evidence. In this case, the science was ancient languages; a science that requires an interest in the lives of those who came before us." Her passion and zeal was infectious, and their eyes began to pick up the glow of her enthusiasm.

"To study the remains of ancient lifestyles," she said, "demands an understanding of the thread that connects all life, regardless of race or origin. As archaeologists, we study the past lives of ancient civilizations because we care about what happened to them, because we know there are lessons to be learned in how they lived and died, and because we realize that except for a small slip in time, they are us.

"Our past holds so many answers. Not just for our everyday curiosity, but what about the great mysteries: Stonehenge, the pyramids of Egypt, the Nazca lines. This accumulated but unexplainable evidence is an undeniable part of our history, compelling us to dig and dive and climb into these lost cultures—because we know that in their everyday lives, they witnessed the creation of wonders we can only dream about. We want to know how they accomplished these miracles."

Gathering steam, she began pacing. "From the Rosetta coin we have the letters of their words, but what is the meaning of those words?"

Carter mouthed, "Say again?" and she ignored him. She looked to Henri, but he busied himself with the contents of his teacup. When she looked at St. Germain, he was rigid in his seat.

She frowned and gave those two a brief snort of disdain, turning back to Carter. "We know their words, Carter, but do we know their meaning? Look at these messages—if we take them chronologically, we start with *You are the Children of Gods.* Then, *Find Your Power in the Greatest Temple.* Now we add the Hebrew message, *Knowledge is the Power. You are the Temple.*"

She looked at all three men, hoping for some glimmer of epiphany, but there was nothing. They stared back at her with carefully held faces. She shrugged and continued.

"So we have two references for temple and two for power. Putting them together it looks like they are saying, '*You are the Children of Gods*—slash—*Find Your Great Power within the Temple that is You.*' "

She pulled a face at her audience. "I hear this sort of drivel from the New Age spiritualists, but it still has no meaning for me. Can anyone tell me what I'm missing?"

Carter shook his head no. Henri turned away so she couldn't see his face. She looked to St. Germain. He squirmed.

"What is your problem?" she asked point blank, coming to sit next to him. "Do you have something you need to share?" She raised her brows and waved her hands expectantly, a magician with a hat waiting for the rabbit to spring up.

When she got no response, she glanced at Carter and his expression warned her to be careful. She returned to St. Germain, and drew back. He leaned forward, reaching for her hands, an explosion of emotional intensity rippling across his face.

"Please, Madelyn," he said. "Are you saying you can translate this language?"

She stared at him for several seconds before her weary brain put it together. When she understood, sudden vertigo swept over her, threatening to topple her. Steadily, she composed her features into a bland look and lightly asked, "Are *you* saying you have something else in this language?"

St. Germain pushed, ignoring her response. "Are

you saying you can translate the symbols?"

"Yes," she replied. She saw the pulse beating at St. Germain's throat jump wildly while his eyes momentarily closed.

"You have no idea," he answered, croaking harshly. Tears filled his eyes when they opened, and his hands shook. "No idea—how long we have waited for you."

Mady froze with anticipation.

Who are "we" and how long have they waited?

"I know this has been a very long and difficult night," St. Germain said. "But I must ask you to stay ... There's a story I'd like to tell."

He smiled and reached for the teapot.

CHAPTER SEVEN

Early Saturday Morning
St. Germain Townhouse
London

St. Germain poured the tea, wondering where to begin.

When Mady said she could read the symbols, the bottom of his heart hit the floor. All his life he had prayed to hear someone say they could read the symbols—and thus, give him answers to relieve him of the life and death dilemma he faced every day—answers that would tell him if his family protected something of immeasurable value ... or not.

Is my family secret really worth dying for?

To challenge the path of his ancestors was unheard of, but he had no choice. He had prayed for answers, and they came.

Do I have the strength to see it through?

He set the teapot down with a surprisingly steady hand. He sat back with a sigh of deep regret that such a day was upon them, for this story had never been told. A quick glance and an encouraging smile from Henri gave him courage.

"Many years ago," he said, "my family became the guardians of something ... very unique that is said to be valuable beyond comprehension. The responsibility for this guardianship has been most difficult."

He stopped and looked at his guests. Both leaned forward in their seats, their faces bewildered, yet attentive. He cleared his throat and continued. "We accepted this difficult task because it first came into the hands of an uncle who was a rich man, very powerful and ... wise."

His voice shook and he paused to sip his tea. His insides were filled with knots. He looked down until Henri rattled his teacup. "This uncle," Solomon continued, "designed the protocol by which we guard this responsibility. He also composed an oath, and a warning."

Again he stopped, his heart pounding. He wanted to gnash his teeth and roll his head with indecision, but the luxury of grief was not his. He was out of time. He glanced at Henri, who stood and moved to the windows giving Solomon distance, allowing him to tell the story. Across from Solomon, Carter and Mady waited with anticipation.

Solomon looked at Mady. "The warning clearly states, 'Reveal only to those who know the meaning of the symbols.' It would seem, Madelyn, you are that person."

She stared back, silent and hesitant. Her eyes were as clear as reflecting pools, urging him to continue.

"Through all the time my family has guarded this ... secret, often upon pain of death—never could anyone decipher the symbols. Nor did we suspect that there were more coins. The coin you saw bearing the Hebrew is one of the pieces that came in a package with the warning."

Mady leaned forward, her brow wrinkled, her expression intense. "So, what is this unique and valuable secret?" She waved her hands in a graceful move, searching for the unknown.

St. Germain answered carefully, balancing his way through the truth. "I don't know," he answered. His voice shook, sounding distressed, even to his ears. He stood. "I've never actually seen what we guard, not all of it. But I do have a copy of the warning and the oath."

Mady pushed her teacup aside and said, "I need coffee. Real American coffee if you have it—black, and lots of it." She shook her head like a rattle and looked at Carter.

"Don't look over here," he said with a shrug. "I'm waiting for you to explain it to me."

She turned back to St. Germain. "I'm sorry, but I'm confused. You say you are guarding something 'upon pain of death,' but you've never seen it?"

St. Germain answered with hooded eyes and a casual shrug. "That part is a long and complicated story. For now you'll just have to trust me."

Mady smothered a curse. Her foot began to flutter as she asked, "What language is the warning in? Do you have it here? May I see it?"

He nodded and walked back to the rear of the room, disappearing again. He returned with a roll of vellum. He released the tie and laid the scroll out on a side table, weighting the corners with onyx statues.

After turning up the light, he ran his hand over the smooth surface. Inside, he quaked, feeling the eyes of countless generations watching him as an unheard-of event loomed.

Please, God, let me do the right thing.

"Come see this, Mady," he called over his shoulder.

She and Carter approached. Just as they neared the table, St. Germain turned, blocking their path and their view. He held his hands out in supplication. "You must know that never in the history of my family has any outsider seen this document. Nor has anyone other than select family members heard the story I just told you."

A pulse jumped madly in his neck and he raised his hand to his throat. "What I am about to do is unprecedented," he said. "I am allowing you to see this because I fear the world has grown too small for me to keep this secret any longer." He saw Mady poised with a thousand questions, but he gave her no opportunity.

He stepped aside, revealing the scroll.

She stared at it for several seconds before looking up at him, her eyes filling her face. "Good Lord, man," she blurted out. "This is old Aramaic. When was it written, and who was your uncle?"

St. Germain drew his shoulders back as the majestic command of three thousand years surrounded him. His voice flowed deep and strong when he spoke. "The original writing is from about 955 BCE. The author, my ancient great-uncle, you would know as King Solomon, Son of David."

•

7:30 AM
Mady's Hotel
Soho

Mason Andrews stood at the hotel desk, impatient. Time was short and they had a blonde to catch.

"Here are your key cards, Mr., uh … Stephens, for

two rooms. We did have one room available on the fifth floor, as you requested. It is the last room, at the end of the hall."

The clerk pushed the key cards toward him. "Shall I ring for someone to help you with your bags?" He peered over the counter at the shortage of luggage.

"No, that won't be necessary," Mason said. He snatched up the key cards and hefted a shabby gray overcoat across his arm. Beneath the coat he carried a brown leather case and a large paper bag. He went straight to the fifth floor stairwell where Greer waited.

"Did you get the rooms like I instructed?" Greer asked.

Mason was eager to make up for his earlier gaff. "Yeah. We got one right next to the girl. The second key card is a great idea. While she's trying to make the wrong card work—" He shrugged and added a feral grin of approval for the simple plan.

They entered the room at the end of the hall. Mason deposited the leather case and coat on the bed while Greer took the paper bag into the adjoining bathroom.

"I'll be ready in five minutes," Greer said, stepping into the small room. He turned about and leveled a gaze at Mason that spoke of no more mistakes. "Sooner or later she'll show up here. You know what they look like, if you spot either one, call me. Now go—and keep your eye out for that gang you claim knocked you out earlier."

Mason ducked his head and slipped out the door, newspaper in hand.

•

St. Germain Townhouse
London

When St. Germain said, "King Solomon, Son of David," Mady rocked back on her heels. Reeling both mentally and physically, she rubbed her eyes to make sure she wasn't hallucinating as well.

King Solomon, son of David? What next?

Behind her, Henri clattered china, returning with a fresh service and the smell of strong Colombian coffee.

Her world was shifting with each new revelation of this long night, leaving her reeling again. Hysterical laughter bubbled within and she fought to suppress it. The ancient message in Aramaic waited for her to read … as she collected her wild thoughts.

The beautiful script on the scroll called to her like a lovely tune she couldn't deny. She stepped to the table and examined the document. The graceful marks danced across the fine vellum, singing, calling her to become a part of something ancient.

"The Warning of Solomon," she read aloud while her fingers hovered, not quite touching it. She looked at St. Germain, who nodded his encouragement. She took a deep breath to steady her quivering vocal chords and read on.

"You will Keep Guardianship over the most powerful knowledge ever given to man," she said. "Keep it safe, upon the forfeit of all lives until the time when man does once again fly with the gods. Reveal this message only to those who know the meaning of the symbols. As God is your witness, swear: I will bear the responsibilities of this legacy, ensuring the safekeeping of this, our family secret. Willingly do I take the Oath and wear the ring of Solomon, understanding the responsibility therein."

Images of a world long past were invoked by the

powerful words. They echoed with a surreal lilt and then settled in the room with a physical presence. She completed the written passage, her voice a soft sweep of reverence. "This I vow for the remainder of my life until my death, incurring jeopardy on my divine spirit upon failure."

She turned to look at Carter. He was collapsed on a nearby settee with his face in his hands.

St. Germain handed her a fresh cup of the aromatic coffee, and the fragrance filled her head, drawing the cobwebs back. She took a hesitant sip of the hot brew and her motor rumbled to life.

"How is this secret ... this knowledge ... connected to us?" she asked. She sat down next to Carter, who was inhaling the scent off a cup of coffee. They watched and listened as St. Germain told his story.

"It was a thousand years before Christ," he said, "when men were Kings, and gods walked the earth." His eloquent voice filled the library, bringing shivers and goose bumps to Mady's flesh.

"First came the wisdom, what some call the Book of Wisdom. Then came the knowledge—what we guard. We can't say how the knowledge reached Solomon. Some have guessed it came with Abraham when he left Ur."

He shrugged, seeking their forgiveness. "We cannot be sure. Even in our family, some details have been lost to antiquity.

"The wisdom gave Solomon the strength and courage to see this secret kept safe until man was ready. In truth, I cannot say if humanity is ready now, for I do not know exactly what 'it' is, even though my family is dedicated to this item's protection." He looked away.

When his eyes came back, Mady saw profound sadness.

"When I see what is being done in the name of man," he said, "I fear we will never 'once again fly with the gods', never earn this legacy so many in my family had died to protect."

He sighed, and Mady recalled the sound of despair from earlier; it came from a battle long-fought. She held her breath and her heart filled with expectation as his story unfolded.

"Whether man is ready or not," St. Germain continued, "I am terrified the knowledge will fall into the hands of those who employ tracking chips and torture. The world, I must concede, has become too small to keep this secret safe any longer—even with St. Germain resources."

He paused to accept his coffee from Henri. While he had chosen to tell them this story, it was obvious to Mady the telling was not easy for him. She sat with Carter, patient and alert, poised once again on the edge of her seat.

"For thirty days," St. Germain continued, "Solomon kept himself in the desert to ponder the gravity of his duty. When he returned, he brought an operating plan for the secret ... whereby guardianship would always rest with three separate family members at any given time.

"One Keeper would know the truth about what it is, but not its location. Another would know the location, but not possess the key, and the Keeper with the key would not know the location."

He shifted in his seat. Mady caught the subtle nod between him and Henri before he continued. "It is a lifetime commitment, and each Keeper selects their successor from the vast international St. Germain family. If something should happen to a Keeper, their part of the secret is privately detailed in their will, which is first disclosed to the other two Keepers.

"In that way, the security of the secret is never the responsibility of a single individual. This protocol has served us well until two months ago.

"At that time, Aunt Ione, the Keeper of the key died. Then, before her replacement could be arranged, Grandpere was murdered. He was the Keeper of the location. That leaves me the only St. Germain Keeper alive. In three thousand years this has never happened."

His face seemed to crumple from the unsustainable weight, confirming the sad truth of his words. "I am afraid the secret and my ability to keep it safe are in dire jeopardy." He paused long enough to pass another quick glance to Henri before rushing on.

"There is something else I wish to show you. It is a message written in the alien script that I believe holds the answers to many of our questions. That is why it was so important to me that you could read the symbols."

Mady stirred and asked, "Is this one of the pieces that came from your ... Uncle Solomon?"

St. Germain nodded yes. Before she could ask more, he added, "Understanding the message is crucial. Because of the two who followed you, I believe we are running out of time. We must move with haste."

At this mention, Carter sat up. "There was only one, and Mady left him for the authorities at the restaurant."

"No, I'm afraid another came while you were out on the bus. When we saw he was waiting for you, we decided to help. Henri took care of him, leaving the man disposed of, out of the way."

Carter reached over and grabbed Mady's hands. "That was close," he said. His eyes were fierce and his brows mashed with worry. "Too close. We have to be more careful."

Mady nodded at Carter's concern, but her mind was already thinking about a translation of the symbols, racing with the possibilities of a message from an extraterrestrial race.

She roused her lagging mental abilities. "Where is this message in the alien script? If I'm going to do anything more complicated, I need my work satchel. We'll have to go back to my room for it."

Immediately, she stood and stretched, turning side-to-side, twisting her back. She held her hand out to Carter, urging him to rise with a challenging flick of her brows. He stood and gave her a slanted look that promised her difficult times ahead.

St. Germain joined Henri near the door. "We will have to go to Surrey, to my country estate," he said. "When Grandpere was killed, I relocated all the pieces to the most secure location I had. We can stop by your hotel on the way."

The four retraced their steps to the Rolls-Royce. Once again Henri took the point position. His dedication to security was both reassuring and sobering.

Once they were seated in the rear of the limo, Carter asked St. Germain, "Tell us about your family members, your Keepers. How did these last two die?"

"The killings actually began centuries ago," St. Germain said. "Every few hundred years, a Keeper would disappear and then turn up with evidence on the body—torture. When we figured out what was happening, we started carrying poison. It is part of what we are willing to do."

He held out his hand, showing them a glittering cabochon ruby with the St. Germain initials embossed in gold. It winked at them, beautiful and deadly in the pale light.

"Aunt Ione consumed her poison. Then Grandpere was taken and was missing for two days when he was found in a Paris alley, dead from a heart attack. He had been tortured. The coroner performed an autopsy and that is how we discovered the tracking chip."

A flash of grief contorted his face. "He was an old man, his heart was weak. He could not have lasted long under such conditions." He stopped to stare at his hand bearing the ruby ring. When he spoke, sadness fell with his words, like tears.

"He was a dear and sweet old man. He should not have died the way he did." His strangled voice broke and he turned away, looking out the window.

Mady reached out and touched St. Germain's arm. "I inherited my coin through my mother," she said. "She and my father just disappeared one day. They were never found, and the mystery of what happened to them never solved."

She glanced up at Carter, needing his steady presence, and was startled by the rippling pain on his face. Alarmed, she asked, "Carter, are you all right?"

His eyes closed, his voice rasped in a whisper. "My mother and father were vacationing in the Swiss Alps, at a little village in the mountains where they had spent their honeymoon. One sunny afternoon they took a sailboat out on the lake. When darkness came and they hadn't returned, a search party went looking for them.

Their bodies were found with the capsized boat. They were drowned—wearing their life vests."

He choked and laughed, his voice rattled as he finished. "Father always was quite the stickler about safety measures." He looked at them and his brows were crucified with pain, even as he struggled to pull a stiff upper lip. "Everyone said it was a freak accident, but I always knew it had something to do with the coin, even though they had no knowledge of it."

Mady's heart constricted at Carter's confession.

His secret.

She looked back and forth between the two men, their faces torn with so much pain. "It seems there is no denying the connection," she said. "Where there are coins, people are dying. We must find out who is doing this and stop them."

•

8:00 AM, Saturday
Mady's Hotel
Soho

The Rolls-Royce stopped in traffic in front of Mady's hotel. She reached for the door handle. "I'll run upstairs while you circle the block. By the time you make one pass, I'll be here waiting for you."

Carter's hand shot out to stop her. "Give me your key," he said. "I'll get your satchel for you. What else do you need?"

She felt her eyes blaze with indignation before she sweetly piped, "Darling, what I need is for you to get out of my way."

She took a moment to glare at him with her best evil eye. "I can handle myself. Didn't I prove that in the restaurant? Look, I won't be intimidated or manipulated, not by them, or you.

"Here, if it makes you feel better, take my spare key card. If I'm not back straight away, you can come up and get me. Relax, I'll be right back."

He opened his mouth for a rebuttal.

"Here, Mady, take this," St. Germain said as he reached into the console between the seats. He removed a cell phone and passed it to her. "Hurry and be careful. All you have to do is hit send."

Mady slipped the phone into the breast pocket of Carter's jacket and jumped out onto the sidewalk. In a flash she slipped through the lobby doors. The lift area was jammed with a crowd of tourists, so she headed for the stairwell.

By the third floor she was cursing in a language man hadn't heard in a thousand years. She reached the fifth floor and pushed the fire door open, her heart pounding from the climb. When she came around the corner and gazed down the long hallway, the premonition she experienced earlier chose this moment to reappear and slip down her spine.

Immediately, her breath stuttered to a stop. The hair on the back of her neck stood up. Ahead of her, the hallway loomed like a gauntlet, seeming alive with evil potential.

She was glad she didn't have to walk the entire hall alone. Her fixed gaze traveled from the end of the threatening hallway to a stooped old man at the door next to hers.

He was a good six inches shorter than she, and his hunched-back body was enveloped in a large gray overcoat. While he didn't appear to be a threat, she was definitely getting a bad feeling.

"Stop it," she admonished, "you're being ridiculous."

She stalked to her room with the key card in hand when the man appeared at her side. She jumped back, startled, dropping her card in the process. She glared at him, ready to pounce at the slightest sign of threat.

"Excuse me, Miss," he said. "I was wondering if you could help me. My arthritis ... I'm having trouble with this little card. Could you?"

He smiled hesitantly and handed her his card.

Mady stood frozen, her inner alarm on full alert. She eyed him—he was old and stooped. In the silence of her hesitation, he bent over, reaching to pick up her dropped card. Against the wall, one of his arthritic hands leaned heavily.

Mady cringed.

Have they made me cold-hearted to a decrepit old man?

He rose with her card in his crippled fingers. She was ashamed for feeling threatened, and her shame squelched her alarms. He smiled from his crooked posture, unable to look up at her, his bent back obviously a torture.

Two seconds, she thought, *is all this will take.*

She took the card from his twisted fingers and he stepped aside, giving her room to pass. She moved to his door and slid the card through the lock—once, twice, three times with no response. She frowned at the key.

Somewhere behind her he was moving, and the hair on the back of her neck jumped up in a wave that shouted, *Run!* She spun, but the gnarled, arthritic fingers were suddenly strong and held a damp cloth. A chemical smell filled her nose as the cloth was shoved into her face. Her legs seemed beyond her control and the ground suddenly swam up to greet her.

Damn it all to—

•

As the Rolls pulled into traffic, Carter looked back at the hotel. He craned his neck to catch a last glimpse of Mady, muttering "Damn Yank." When Mady slipped from sight, he turned on St. Germain. "You were out of line," he spit. "I didn't want her to go alone. You are in no position to interfere."

St. Germain held his hand out, and said, "Easy, Carter, I had to talk to you alone. We only have a moment and I need to know … where you stand on what we are dealing with. If necessary, I intend to see this business finished today. I have to know if you're in all the way."

Carter scrubbed his face. His energy reserves had long ago expired, leaving him barely able to keep up, much less think ahead. He gave St. Germain a hard look. The man obviously anticipated a confrontation with their pursuers—soon.

Could he find it within his deeply cultured convictions to kill someone? Carter sat back, his fists knotted. This was the implication he got from St. Germain. He thought of his mother and ground his teeth. Then he pictured Madelyn as he first saw her at Marsten Hall, so magnificent in iridescent blue silk. He stared at St. Germain and the seconds ticked by.

"What about the authorities?" Carter argued, unable to squelch the voice of reason. "Shouldn't we be calling them in, before we discuss anything so drastic as what you're saying. I mean, do you really think we'll have to—"

St. Germain reached down into his briefcase. He pulled out a photograph from the Paris morgue and laid it in Carter's lap. "Do you want to go home, leaving the authorities to find who did this?"

Carter stared at the photograph with morbid curiosity. He saw what they did to the old man, and he closed his eyes, unable to imagine how dreadful that had been for him. In the face of such brutality, Carter's cultured convictions ran like honey in the sun, giving way to a powerful ferocity to save those he loved from such horrors.

There is no turning back.

In confirmation to this thought, his head nodded back and forth. St. Germain misread, and hissed with disappointment, but Carter pressed on. "No, do not mistake me. I have no problem with what you suggest. You can count me in. Whatever it takes."

Catching St. Germain's eye he finished with a hard look and a gentleman's nod of confirmation. "Yes, whatever it takes."

St. Germain looked forward where Henri's eyes met his.

"Good," he said, seeing they had come around the last corner. "Then together we will see it done."

They pulled up to the curb in front of the hotel and looked for Mady's long-legged form.

She was nowhere in sight.

•

Mady struggled away from the suffocating darkness, gasping for air, screaming for light, begging to live. She felt restriction clinging to her body and she tried to kick it away, but it wrapped around her hands and her feet.

Suddenly the cloying darkness turned to gray, the

gray separated into colors, and the colors became a face. She forced her eyes into focus, staring at an unknown visage speaking soundlessly. She cocked her head and blinked—and then her ears roared back to life.

"—a new experimental drug those boys in the lab cooked up. One little whiff and you're out like a stone. Then it dissipates through the lungs and you're back on line—"

At this point, the face looked down and a watch came into Mady's peripheral vision. "—in three minutes and forty-eight seconds," the face droned.

Just as she started to wrinkle her forehead in confusion, clarity rocked through her consciousness with a sudden swoop that knocked her stomach flat.

The little old man!

Only he was not so little any more. The stooped back was now straight, the beard and moustache on the floor next to the theatrical gloves that made his fingers look ruined. Mady slumped and bit back a curse, wondering if the safety of her room was next door.

I should have listened to Carter.

She looked up and the man grasped her chin with rough fingers. When he gave her head a sharp little jiggle, her brain scrambled, fanning her disorientation. She glared at him, committing his face to eternal memory.

He was tall, with dark hair and an American accent, but the rest of his features were nondescript. His eyes were light, but she couldn't say if they were gray, blue, or green. Although he was of a medium build, his grip on her face was like steel. His skin was pale, as though he never saw the light of day. His voice made her flesh crawl, even before she understood what he was saying.

"I know you're alert in there, so don't bother playing possum. First you should understand that if you try anything stupid, you will regret it. Second, know that I have a score to settle with you ... understand?"

She nodded. While he frightened her, there was a soft chord in his voice that belied his words. The mystery of this discrepancy set bells of alarm ringing in her heart. She didn't want to know this man. She didn't want to know how he knew her, did not want to understand why there was a score between them in need of settling.

"Now, I'm going to remove the tape on your mouth, and ask you some questions. You will answer these questions to the best of your ability, immediately, because I am an impatient man this morning. If you do not cooperate, I will exercise any number of unpleasant options upon your person."

He waved a small vial before her face, catching her eyes. "I may give you another dose of the drug you just received, and during the three minutes and forty-eight seconds you are out, I can work on settling our score.

"Or I may give you a different drug, also from those boys in the lab. They assure me you will then gladly tell me everything you know. Oh, perhaps I should explain: there are some rather nasty residual effects from this drug, but what the hell, it's your body, not mine." He shrugged, nonchalant.

Mady pressed back into her chair. She could not get away. When he looked at her, he sneered with a depravity she didn't know was possible. She desperately didn't want to hear any more, yet he continued.

"Or, I could open up my little packet of surgical tools and see what body parts you're willing to give up, but that always gets kind of messy." He shook his head and wrinkled his nose with distaste. "Such a pretty girl ... you don't want to go there."

She shivered as his words enveloped her, going beyond her ears to seep into her heart and mind, contaminating her with his ugliness. Her eyes watered and her bravado turned to smoke. He didn't need to do all this to entice her cooperation. Bound and gagged, she quivered with helpless fear and unmitigated rage, ready to confess anything if he would just release her—so she could kill him.

Who is he, and what does he know?

The answers were too ominous. She back-pedaled, her heart thudding irregularly.

Something unbearable my way comes.

She didn't want to know.

The man reached for her face and she drew back, cringing. He jerked the tape from her mouth, leaving the delicate skin irritated. She worked her jaw to see if she could still speak. When she felt capable, she looked up at him and nodded.

"What are you and Carter up to?" he asked.

Not knowing where to start, she mistakenly shook her head no. Before she could explain, the cloth returned to her face and she was gone.

She came to and immediately noticed he had been busy in the last three minutes and forty-eight seconds. The chair she was bound to now sat beside a small table with a lamp. In the pale light, she saw a brown leather case opened to display two smaller black cases.

One of the black cases was open and she saw a pair of plastic wrapped syringes and a small vial.

Ah, the drug with the unsavory, residual side effects.

She gulped and licked lips that tasted of adhesive before realizing she had no moisture in her mouth. And there was still another small black case yet to open.

He winked, reading her mind, and opened the remaining case.

When she saw the contents her teeth came together. He began laying out the tools and Mady knew hysteria was a breath away. Full throttle panic sprouted in her gut, alive and hungry, poised to begin gnawing on her. With morbid efficiency, she catalogued his little black bag of horrors.

First, the predictable sharp, curved dental tool. At first sight of it, her dry mouth decided to fill with water.

Next she spied a scalpel with a glittering razor edge that needed no introduction. Beside that were two tools she didn't recognize, and didn't want to know.

She moved her gaze to the next frightening piece.

Pale light glinted off the razor sharp edge of a cigar clipper. Mady closed her eyes and curled her toes and fingers into tight little balls. She wanted to throw her head back—to moan and thrash against her bindings with mindless rage.

But that wouldn't make this awful man go away.

She fought for control. She couldn't help herself tied up. If she wanted to get loose, she had to convince this guy of her cooperation. She snapped her eyes open.

He pulled a chair around in front of her and sat, picking up the cigar clipper, toying with it. His voice was surprisingly soft and soothing.

"I understand these relationships can sometimes get off to a rocky start, so let me contribute something of my expertise. Perhaps that will save us a little time and grief."

He winked again. In spite of his earlier claim of being impatient, they were now comrades enjoying a moment. She watched him set the cigar tool down and extend his hand out over the table, letting it hover above the two little cases of horror.

Sick fascination consumed her as his hand floated with maddening grace—back and forth, back and forth. At last he settled over one of the tools she didn't recognize and he made to pick it up.

He stopped mid-motion when they heard Carter enter her room next door. They could hear him call out her name. "Mady—"

Mady's comrade held one finger up to his mouth. "Sssshhh." From out of his waistband came a large caliber handgun. He held it up in front of her face as he attached a silencer. "Call out to him, and he will die, understand?"

She clamped her lips together in a posture of silence. They listened, heads cocked, until they heard the door bang shut. After a few seconds of silence, they heard Carter no more. He left her room with a distinct slamming of the door.

Mady exhaled with relief. "What do you want to know?"

"I want you to tell me what you and Nicholas Carter have been doing since you arrived at his house last night?"

She had no doubt he would find out everything she knew, with or without her cooperation. Things were spinning too fast.

What part did he want to know? Where did she start? What could she tell him without divulging enough to earn her quick demise?

His hand began to twitch back and forth between the two cases and she knew she had to say something soon. She gulped and opened her mouth—

The cell phone in Carter's jacket pocket rang.

CHAPTER EIGHT

Mady flinched in her seat as far as her bindings would allow. The ringing cell phone echoed in her ears, synchronizing with the pounding of her heart.

Cripes! They're going to kill me off with a heart attack before this guy starts his torture.

She glared at the man as he reached into her pocket and grabbed the phone. He jammed the end of the silencer under her chin, pushing her head back. "Say hello," he whispered, placing the phone to her ear.

At his nod, Mady squeaked, "Hello."

"Darling, what's taking you so long? We really need to get going," Carter said.

The man with the gun whispered, "Carter?" When she nodded yes, he took the phone.

"Mr. Carter, this is Jack Greer. It seems I have something of yours." He stood close to Mady and stroked her hair with the hand that held the gun. He bent down and smiled, giving her a wink while he talked. "Can you tell me why I should return her to you?"

She couldn't hear Carter's response, but Greer looked into her face and mouthed the word "artifact," grinning broadly. He held the phone behind him and whispered to her, "What kind of artifacts do you have?"

She clamped her lips tight and glared back at him with an obstinate thrust of her chin. The thought of Carter being close roused her bravado. Greer tapped her soundly on the temple with the silencer, making her eyes water.

"Why would I be interested in a dusty old artifact," he said to Carter, "when I already have your pretty little girl?" Carter's lengthy response came, his voice sounding like a little tin man. Greer stood up, interested, his lips pursed in a silent whistle.

Mady watched him, and a great fear for all of them swelled in her chest. As bad as this man was, he must answer to someone even worse.

"Café Dolce, on Boyle Street," Greer said. "Be there before I arrive in ten minutes. You will sit at the counter with an open newspaper—alone."

The cell phone was snapped shut. He stood giving Mady a long, hard look, making her squirm in her seat. Finally, he pulled off a new length of tape and smoothed it across her mouth, this time his touch was surprisingly gentle.

He turned to leave, took two steps, then stopped to stare at her again, holding a finger to his mouth ... obviously trying to remember something. Mady went still, as if to disappear, and stared back—her blue eyes locked onto his pale ones. Like an animal, she would gladly chew through a limb if it would give her an escape. But trapped, all she could do was stare.

A veil of sadness fell across his pale eyes and she knew when he remembered what it was he was trying to recall. Tears burst in the back of her eyelids while her heart lodged painfully against her ribs, yet she glared at him with as much ferocity as she could muster.

This man knows about my parents.

This she knew, just as surely as if he had spoken the words. Sick curiosity turned her to stone. She just wanted to kill him before he got a chance to say what he knew.

He stopped at the door and made a call. "Mason, I need you to come up here and sit with the blonde. I'm going to get her boyfriend. Hurry."

•

Downstairs in the hotel lobby, Solomon St. Germain lounged against an enclosed phone booth. "Carter, be still in there. I promise you we will find her ... and we will get her back safe and sound. Please, trust me."

Casually, St. Germain followed the random movements of everyone in the lobby while he called Henri on his cell. "*Oui*, Café Dolce," he said on his cell phone. "*Sur Boyle, au comptoir avec un journal ouvert.*"

He pocketed the phone and whispered to Carter, "Henri will draw off the man, Greer, so we can locate Mady. My guess is that he has an accomplice down here somewhere, probably looking for you."

"Time is wasting, St. Germain, they could be doing—"

"Carter, I don't need you to remind me what they could be doing. The GPS on the cell phone tells us she is somewhere in the hotel, but where would you go to rescue her?"

Precious seconds passed before St. Germain whispered, "*Voilá*, the man from the second Renault, I see him."

The man that St. Germain watched rose, closed a cell phone and walked straight to the lift.

"The stairs," St. Germain whispered. "He has pressed the button for the fifth floor."

Carter exited the booth and fell in step behind St. Germain. They slipped into the stairwell and bounded up to the sixth floor where they stopped and waited, watching the doorway below. Carter paced, fretting, while St. Germain counted down two minutes on his Rolex. They heard the door open down below followed by hurried steps going down.

"All right, there he goes," St. Germain whispered. "Now, let's find Mady and get her back."

They entered the stairwell and ran down to the fifth floor. Peeking around the corner, St. Germain surveyed the empty hallway.

•

Mady sat up when Greer's accomplice entered the room. Instant trepidation set her heart on the fly. With one look, she knew he was going to hurt her. The other man, Greer, was a killer—but this guy liked hurting people, and wore that desire like a badge.

All she knew was she had to get out before he hurt her.

They whispered, tossing an occasional glance her way. The second man jerked a thumb in her direction and she heard him say, "She looks familiar. Didn't we—"

"Shut up, you fool," Greer hissed, delivering a threatening look. "I shouldn't be gone more than twenty minutes. Keep her quiet till I get back. And don't do anything stupid." He shot a quick glance at her, adding, "Don't touch her—I mean it."

Greer gave her a long speculative look, his pale eyes glittering with busy thoughts she could only guess. He turned and left before Mady could ask if she could go with him.

Sure, then maybe he can take us out for ice cream.

As soon as the door closed after Greer, the big man, Mason, turned on her. She trembled. Foaming madness rose and waved from a corner of her mind, confident she would arrive in good time. She ground her teeth and focused on the sticky bite of tape against her bare ankles and the madness drew back. In its place, a chilling paralysis spread through her limbs.

Mason came toward her, staring a little too hard. Trapped in the chair, she was helpless to stop his perusal. He stood directly in front of her, so close his cologne gagged her behind the tape.

Suddenly he moved, fast as a predator, bringing the heat and moisture of his breath roaring into her face. Without warning, he licked her cheek in a long, slow sweep with the full flat of his tongue. When he reached her cheekbone, his tongue disappeared, replaced by his rapidly sniffing nose.

Sniff, sniff—like a dog on the scent, he inhaled her face. Sated with her smell, he exhaled a long, "Ahhhhh." He stood before her, inspecting her, insulting her, and invading her all in one evil sweep of his eyes. Mady stared back, her rage filling her face with a well of fatal retribution.

"Got something to say?" he asked. His smile was smug and sure as he grabbed the tape and freed her mouth with a quick snap. The tape parted from her skin with a rip.

She choked, trying to breath and spit at the same time. A demonic desire for his death possessed her and she dared him with her hot eyes, snarling and hissing.

"You can't do this to people, there are laws—"

He laughed and pressed the tape back over her mouth. Leaning down into her mute face, he mocked her. "Right now, baby, I am the law ... and I can do whatever I want."

Mady closed her eyes and squeezed them as tight as she could, but his laughter and his words surrounded her. Tears of utter helplessness stabbed her eyelids as he spoke.

"Now I know why you look familiar," he said.

He walked around her, disappearing behind her. When she felt him sniff at her head, her scalp crawled from where his warm breath touched her flesh. When he lifted the hair at her nape, a tear rolled down her cheek.

An eternity passed before he reappeared on her opposite side, breathing straight into her ear. Her toes curled tight inside her sneakers and she hunched forward, preparing for whatever came next.

"I knew her," he said. "Your mother."

Mady's spine shot straight up and her head drew back, her eyes wide open. Her bound hands flexed and gripped the chair with fingers like talons. All the hate she could harness came pouring from her eyes.

"We actually became very close," he said.

He nodded with memory, generating a second tear to roll down Mady's cheek. He reached out and touched her face, collecting the tear on his fingertip. "I think you and I could be close, too. Too bad she's not here to join us."

Slowly, he put the finger to his lips and sucked. "It was your smell that made it for me—you smell just like her ... and your tears taste the same too."

Mady squeezed her eyes shut. *Too much, too much.*

She couldn't take any more. She fled to the bleakest, farthest place in her mind—but his laugher and his words followed her. He whispered obscenities about her mother, baiting her, wanting her to open her eyes. But the vision his words painted scorched her very soul. When she could no longer stand the horror of his words within her mind—

She opened her eyes.

He was face to face with her—so close she breathed his exhalation. There was no escape for her—no way for her not to absorb the horrors this man had committed upon her mother.

She focused on his mouth, opening and closing incessantly until her brain shut down, refusing to process another word. His speech and movements slowed to a pinpoint. Time stopped, giving her respite, a moment of being neither here nor there.

Then the slow motion exploded as if shot from a rubber band. A torrent of retribution was born in her heart and flowed streaming all the way to her fingertips. She wrapped around this rage until her entire being coalesced into a single, driven thought.

This monster must die.

Her earlier impassioned plea to Carter about the sanctity of life dissipated in the flash of this all-consuming desire. Fresh and vibrant on the brilliant screen of her mind came a single dot of red, pulsing into an explosion of darkness. All of her misery—the grief, the despair and the loneliness that came out of the loss of her parents, came boiling and festering in a wave, riding over her, through her, consuming her.

And then it was gone.

She blinked, again and again, as tumblers fell into

place in her mind with an answer she would have never thought possible. The rage and hatred had conceived and delivered something previously unknown into her heart: a promise to her retribution. She nodded in welcome.

Beneath the tape, her lips tightened into a smile.

•

"They do not have room service here, St. Germain," came Carter's insistent words.

"Then we pray Mady's kidnapper does not know. Now stand along the wall out of sight. I will be the waiter. Your face is too well known. Remember—let me hit him with the tayser first."

St. Germain buttoned his jacket. "If there is more than one, we may be in trouble, so stay sharp. We must get her out of there before Greer comes back. Ready?"

They stepped up to the door at the end of the hall. Carter took his position and St. Germain rapped on the door.

"Room service," he called.

•

Mady stared at the big man, forcing herself to stay still. She knew there was no room service

Carter, God bless you, you're here.

Mason grinned and asked her, "Greer ordered food?" He called over his shoulder, "Leave it by the door." They heard a rustling in the hallway, then silence. He turned his attention back to her and she gave him blank eyes.

The knock came again. "Room service."

"Damn it," Mason growled. He stomped to the door in angry strides, his face flushed. He glanced back at her before looking through the peephole. "Dumb Pakistani," he cursed. He jerked the door open like a shot, and hissed, "I said—" Before he could finish, the door burst inward and he dropped to the floor in a writhing, jerking mass.

Carter rushed in behind St. Germain, and Mady sagged with relief. She stared at the man on the floor, now rendered harmless ... and knew there was a God.

Sweet vengeance mine.

She squealed and jerked at her bindings, thumping the chair with insistence. Carter came running and removed the tape from her hands.

"All right now," he said, trying to soothe her.

Behind him, St. Germain bound the man on the floor, applying the tape with abandon before he and Carter hefted him onto the bed. He lay face down with his head turned to the wall.

Mady pulled the last of the tape from her ankles and jumped out of the chair. She erupted into a mad dance, squealing and scrubbing frantically at her face and hair. She shook and shimmied, insane with needing to erase any remnants of the man's touch. At last she came to a halt, panting.

Oblivious of Carter and St. Germain, Mady, her hair wild across her face from her crazy dance of revulsion, and with a primal sound rumbling from deep in her throat, stared at the man on the bed. Now helpless, as she had been only moments ago, and a prisoner, he was hers. She walked toward the bed, remembering the monster's words.

St. Germain's arm shot out, blocking her.

Without taking her eyes from the man on the bed, she ground out. "I need a minute."

"We have to go," he said tersely.

"You'll have to wait," she answered.

They stood face to face, Mohammed and the Mountain, each implacable. St. Germain stood his ground, staring into her eyes, the same calm and open blue eyes he had examined only hours ago.

Mady knew he would not see the same eyes.

Seconds passed, and St. Germain stepped aside to stand with Carter. Together they watched.

Mady sat down next to the man who had licked her face only minutes earlier. His head was turned so that she had to lean over him to see his face. When she saw he was alert, she touched him.

One gentle hand rested on his forehead and caressed his hair, carefully pushing the strands from his watering eyes. She wanted him to be able to hear and see her clearly. She placed her lips by his ear. "So, I guess you're not the law anymore, are you?"

He tried to react, but his stunned nervous system left him capable of little more than random, spasmodic jerks. He was helpless, as she had been earlier. Tears and snot ran down his face. He pleaded silently.

She stood and fixed her feet in a solid stance, bending over him. She spoke for his ears only. "If I go to hell for sending you there first, it will be worth it." With sure precision she placed one knee firm against his neck and one hand on his forehead. She took a deep breath and jerked his head upward.

The sound of his snapping neck bones filled the silence.

Mady's shoulders slumped. There was no time for remorse, even if she had any. She closed her eyes and gave three good breaths. What she did was the one move her parents never had.

She squared her shoulders, giving a quick glance to

the instruments on the table. No, there was no remorse, and she was glad. She looked at Carter and St. Germain. With a wave of her hand toward the body on the bed, she said, "I had to."

Carter gave a fast glance to the table. "No one is questioning you."

St. Germain spoke softly. "Well done, Madelyn."

She nodded, needing them to understand.

Carter stepped to her side. "Anyone would have done the same." He offered a shaky smile, and she sagged into the relief of his sheltering arms.

St. Germain grabbed his cell phone from the table. "Now, we really must go," he said. "The other man will return soon. We'll leave this mess for him to clean up."

Carter opened the door and peeked out into the hallway. He gave the signal and they made straight for the stairs. On the second floor they found an employee lift to the basement. From there a delivery door released them into the cool morning fog.

Mady burst through the door and took to the streets with a sob of relief. Her knees wobbled and she swiped at her eyes and cheeks. Never in her life did she suspect herself capable of what she just did upstairs.

But then, never had she encountered such evil.

Suddenly she remembered her satchel and stopped, causing Carter to run full into her. She wailed, "My work satchel—I never made to my room to get it. Carter, I must have it if I'm going to do a translation. We have to go back."

"It's all right, Mady, we have it," he said. "I grabbed it when I was in your room. It's in the limo, waiting for you."

"How did you know where I was?" she asked, fresh

tears of relief gathering. "How did you find me? I could have been anywhere in the city."

St. Germain came to where they stood and collected an arm from each, towing them along.

"The cell phone, *cherie*, has a locator programmed into it. As soon as you answered the call, we knew you were in the hotel. I recognized the man in the lobby, but it was Carter who spotted a button from your sweater by the door." He shrugged his shoulder gallantly. "The rest you know."

Mady's legs quivered. She didn't regret what she did, but thanks to the words of a stranger, something in her was lost. She was too exhausted to think about it. "Where are we going now?" she asked. "Why are we on foot?"

"We go to rendezvous with Henri," answered St. Germain. "While we were collecting you, my cousin has been entertaining the man named Greer."

St. Germain led them to a small park off Lexington Street. The great Rolls sat purring with Henri lounging against the front fender. When he saw them, he smiled brightly, and called out, "*Bon jour*, miss. Welcome back."

He opened the door and they fell inside. Mady watched St. Germain walk around the car with his cousin and the two talked. Henri was waving his hands and laughing, shaking his head. They whispered one more time before St. Germain climbed into the back seat.

Mady sighed, utterly exhausted. Her adrenaline spent, she sagged into Carter's warmth. It must be her British genes falling down on the job again.

Carter put his arm around her and hugged her close. Placing his mouth against her hair, he inhaled her essence, much the way the other man had. But this time she shivered with joy and relief.

"I thought I'd lost you," he whispered into her scalp, sending a rash of goosebumps down her neck. "I won't let it happen again."

She wiggled down into the warmth and comfort of his arm, relishing the safety of his presence. When she finally settled, Carter asked St. Germain, "We go to your country estate?"

"Yes," St. Germain said. "We go to Chateau la Roche. There, you will see the secret of King Solomon."

•

10:30 AM
London

Sitting at his desk, Jack Greer pinched the bridge of his nose, and mumbled. "What a frickin' mess."

He dragged his head from side to side, pulling on his neck till it popped. "Oohhh," he groaned. He hadn't had a decent night's sleep in weeks—maybe months. Now this. Thank God he was able to sanitize the hotel room before Scotland Yard arrived. He looked at the crime scene photos.

Mason Andrews, his eyes vacant and crystallized, stared up from a head facing backward.

Sorry, 'ol buddy, but you deserved this.

"I hope the girl did it," Greer mumbled with little satisfaction. He rolled his head from side to side again. Tight muscles or not, he thought, "At least my face is still on the front side." He left the desk and stared out at the endless underground storage surrounding him.

"Walk away," whispered the voice of madness inside his head. "Just leave, you can do it."

The absurdity of his insanity was, in all, a marvel.

He chuckled. "Not only do I have nightmares, but now I hear voices, too." His chuckle withered to a strangled choke.

Surrounding him were endless rows of files. Did he really believe there was anything from his life that wasn't recorded, probably somewhere in this very room?

He turned away.

Despite his best efforts, everything with this case was going straight to hell—and there was nothing he could do about it. While he did his best to frighten the girl without hurting her, he hated to think about what that sick bastard Mason did to get his head flipped around.

Wildcard or not, this foul-up with Mason was out of the bag; there was nothing Greer could do to fix it now. Still, he shouldn't have let it happen, shouldn't have let things spiral out of control like this.

The remnants of his chuckle soured in his mouth. There would be no retirement, no fishing in Oregon, and he knew it. He exhaled with a rush, seeing his hopes fade to impossible. He had been foolish to think there was an escape from this life-long employment.

No one who has ever seen The One lives to talk about it.

The special phone on his desk waited—he couldn't put it off any longer. With reluctant fingers, he dialed the number.

He waited while a receptionist and two assistants held him in limbo, like a worm on a hook, twisting in the breeze, waiting for the first bite to land. Finally, he heard the telltale click. He licked his dry lips as the voice of terror spoke his name.

"Jack Greer, do you have good news for me?" The

One asked.

Greer cleared his throat and announced, "I'm afraid I have a situation." He pressed on. "I have two names for you, both in archaeology: Nicholas Alexander Carter and Madelyn Rose Fox. The woman was implanted three years ago. Last night about midnight she was in the company of Mr. Carter when the implant was discovered, removed and disposed of."

Greer heard the beginning of a hiss from the other end and kept talking, hoping to finish before it escalated into something worse. "An operative was placed, but there was—contact. That operative is now being detained by the local authorities."

The hiss became a snarl and Greer closed his eyes, thankful this was a phone report and not a personal delivery. "A second agent," he hurried, "was placed and the woman apprehended. I was unsuccessful in acquiring her companion and when I returned, the woman was gone and the agent left in charge was deceased."

The snarl grew into a rumbling growl, forcing Greer to shrink back in his chair. He pressed on to finish. "Presently their whereabouts are unknown, but I do have a partial on the vehicle of an apparent third party. We are conducting a search now. I hope to have a name and an address within the hour." Just as he finished, the sweat began to pop out on his brow.

His heart was a battering ram while he waited for a response.

And waited. And waited.

The bile in his stomach began to curdle. The silence stretched, smothering him. His breath sat stalled in his chest.

He imagined invisible fingers wrapped around his

neck—squeezing tighter and tighter until his breath filled his throat and his lungs were ready to burst. He leaned forward, certain he heard the first hiss as the sword of Damocles came for his miserable neck.

"Do you have anything else at this time?" said the voice.

Greer's heart lurched in his chest and he gasped like a landed perch. An insane urge to request a sabbatical for the purpose of taking up religion flitted through his heart. He swallowed the thought with a gurgle of relief. "No sir," he replied.

"Then you will collect the appropriate files and report back to me when you have a name. Call me then, priority one, understand?"

The sword lifted and swung away. Greer's miserable neck was intact—for the moment. "Yes sir," he said, wiping the sweat from his face.

•

On the Road to Surrey

St. Germain watched the busy streets pass by as Henri navigated the Rolls through the crowded city. They crossed the River and headed south into the country, to the unimaginable, the inevitable.

Time is running out. I must know—I have to decide.

He quaked at the thought of what he was about to do, but events seemed destined to push him toward this decision. As inevitable as this conclusion seemed, he wasn't sure if he could go through with it.

Carter's voice interrupted his thoughts and St. Germain brought his attention to the present.

"What can you tell us about this alien message and these pieces?" Carter asked.

St. Germain glanced to the front of the limo, but this time Henri's eyes were not there. Again, this decision was Solomon's, as was the story. "There are four pieces in the package that came from King Solomon. The warning of Solomon that Mady read is a copy of the original."

He stopped to clear his throat and fumbled to open a center console, drawing out a chilled bottle of water. He cracked the seal and drained an Evian. "Please, excuse my manners," he said, waving his hand at the console. "Help yourself."

Mady nodded and reached to take one. "We'll share, thanks. Please go on, I'd like to hear more."

"Besides the coin, there is also ... an ebony box." He stuttered, struggling to not say what he had to say. "The box is ... is covered in the alien symbols. The fourth piece is a key to the box—we think."

Carter and Mady stared at him, their mystified faces sagging from fatigue.

St. Germain shrugged with true remorse. "You will understand when you see the artifacts. Many have tried, but no one has been able to open this box." Feeling his own weariness, he added, "Beyond that, it is our assumption and our ... belief that the box contains the knowledge—somehow."

Mady shifted in her seat. "So, you have no idea at all what you have been keeping." Amazed, she said, "The dedication your family has maintained to this responsibility is phenomenal—and all of it from sheer faith. How did this burden come to you?"

"King Solomon returned from the desert knowing blood was the strongest bond for such a responsibility, and so he looked within his family for the first Keeper of this knowledge. In his wisdom he knew the secret must go with a woman, for a man's nature would eventually put the knowledge in peril."

He looked at Mady as though the story were about her. "Solomon examined the lives of the women and realized what amazing strength they possessed. While man destroys, women build homes and live to start another day.

"He chose his half-sister, Tamar, who had been raped as a child. Where other women would have become bitter over such circumstances, Tamar flourished, using her beauty and intellect to create a new life in spite of the tragedy.

"She found great love with a man who would have been below her station as a princess. But, as a soiled woman, she was free to marry outside the royal constraints. Tamar embraced her new role as the wife of a merchant and prospered. When her husband passed on, she retained control of the business and continued to increase her wealth. She was very successful, respected and admired.

"This was the spirit Solomon needed. He chose her to help him create the empire he envisioned: a family dynasty, separate from the House of David, with a global and financial reach sufficient enough to support the secret indefinitely.

"Tamar and her children were relocated in Greece, invested with a great treasure from Solomon for the purpose of taking the knowledge away and keeping it safe. That is where the St. Germain family began.

"From that time, we have been very prosperous, in both wealth and power, as Solomon wanted. The St. Germain family is on every continent and in every business possible, following an edict from Tamar that has served us well over the millennia. She advised us to 'hide in plain sight' and 'be diverse.' Her words were very wise."

"When did the killings begin?" Mady asked.

"The first death that mobilized us," St. Germain said, "was in the late eleventh century during the crusades. That slain Keeper passed the truth on to his daughter. She infiltrated the Knights Templar organization by marrying a son of one of the nobles in Hugh de Payan's entourage. Through this connection the secret was moved to Europe, with new branches of the family starting in France and England.

"We further expanded our wealth through our connections with the Templar banking system. By the time the Templars were disbanded, we were already disengaged from them. However, there was another Keeper murdered in 1335, so we decided that a new secret organization was needed."

Carter and Mady both sat alert. Like children with a good bedtime story, they leaned forward. St. Germain smiled, proud of his family's history.

"A St. Germain patriarch used his power and influence to begin a new organization. Based on original family records, he designed this new organization after an ancient cult from the time of King Solomon.

"This organization was designed to re-affirm our commitment to the legacy. It was dedicated to the honor and integrity of King Solomon's court and is still in existence. They are the Freemasons, and they have upheld their high standards admirably.

"Before World War I, we moved the secret to America, but then it was returned to the continent two years ago."

St. Germain paused, drawing a deep breath. He was surprised at how easy the story went once he got started. "And now my friends, you know as much as I do," he said. "The great mystery remains—what do the symbols say, and who is after us?"

He turned to Mady with a prayer of hope in his heart, aware of how vulnerable they all were. "When I show you the alien writing, how quickly can you to translate it?"

Mady lifted her work satchel. "My notes," she said as she pulled out a laptop, "are actually a software program I developed for working with the symbols.

"With what I learned from deciphering your Rosetta coin message, I just need to make a few adjustments. Then all I have to do is enter the symbols and the program churns out the translation. It's as quick as data entry."

"That's good," St. Germain said, "because I am afraid we have run out of time. When Henri made his escape from the man at the bakery, it is probable our license plate was seen. We must expect them soon."

He exhaled with grief. "My friends, I must apologize for putting your lives in danger. But I cannot tell you how good it is to have you beside me. The decision I face is too much for one man to make alone." He saw the weariness in their faces and regretted what he must ask of them.

"You have been through a great deal, but I have to know what the alien message is. Translate the writing, Madelyn, then we will try to open the box … and see this power my family has been dying to protect for three thousand years."

He tried to smile and couldn't, for his heart grieved over his next words. Pressing his palms together in supplication, he said, "I think it is time to decide if this knowledge, this power my family has kept secret for thousands of years, is truly worth dying for."

CHAPTER NINE

"Madelyn Rose Fox, Nicholas Alexander Carter, Madelyn Rose Fox, Nicholas Alexander ..."

In the war room of his great chateau, Maelstrom purred like a big Chrysler engine in overdrive. "What do they have?" he asked.

Over and over their names churned endlessly through his mind, as he searched for the lock that would accommodate the key that was their names. While there were countless names in his vast memory, spanning so many centuries, he was undaunted. He knew he would find it—he always did.

"Searching through history via the archaeologists was a good plan," he said. Certain this current event held the answers he sought, he nodded, as certain as he knew his own name.

Maybe this is what I have searched for all these millennia.

"I was right," he said, rumbling with pleasure. "The ancient alien race that came before us must have left more behind, some technology yet to be discovered. No matter what the aliens left, I want it."

That extraterrestrial race that came to earth before Maelstrom fascinated him from the very beginning. His first sight of the Great Pyramid clearly told him such perfection did not come from the primitive people of this planet.

Who were the others? Where did they come from? What was their purpose here? Even more important, did they leave behind something he could use to save himself from a life wasted on this miserable planet?

He thrummed his fingers against the table in agitation, lost within his vast and ancient memory. His arrival to this planet was a mistake, an accident of space travel. His kind, only twelve in all, stumbled onto earth in a damaged craft.

"Ahh," he moaned. He shook his head at the mystery of it, regretting all that had ultimately come to loss—all that had been destroyed on that day—all that was beyond replacement.

Namely, his life as it should have been. How often he had wondered about his coming here. How often he had thought, was he here purely by accident, or was he playing a part in some great design?

They had been fortunate enough to land in Egypt—in the midst of a society that worshipped a race of gods—giants with incredible powers who came from the sky in great flying chariots.

"Ha!" He barked his laugh, and his big hands curled into hammer fists. That day was burned into his memory with unstinting clarity—how the little people fell to their knees, chattering in their simple language. While their words were unknown, their actions were clear to Maelstrom's kin.

Quickly they realized, with an uncertain future before them, the rich potential of the moment. He and his brothers could not pass it up. They took their best option and became gods.

They were surprised how easy it was.

He released one great fist and spread the fingers wide. It was a hand that could wrap around a human throat, able to end a life with little more than a squeeze, a hand capable of taking whatever he desired.

His fingers resumed their thrumming as he remembered how his life as a god began. As extraterrestrials, their normal physical abilities were extraordinary to the people of this planet, making them appear as gods.

But it was their unique DNA that truly made them godlike—giving Maelstrom's kind indefinite life spans, allowing them to move on to successive civilizations, amassing incredible wealth and power over the millennia.

"We were the gods to so many," he ruminated.

For almost four thousand years his species had guided and influenced the people of this planet. The last thousand years alone were a product of Maelstrom's solitary ruthless hand.

But even as a god, it seems, I have run out of time.

Radiation from this sun was degrading his DNA, destroying its ability to regenerate. For all his accumulated wealth and power, for all the millennia of manipulation, his destiny, delivered neatly on that fateful day, remained unchanged after all this time.

"I am as doomed today as I was four thousand years ago."

His hand stopped its nervous movement and he returned to repeating the names. "Fox and Carter, Carter and Fox ..."

Whatever they were up to, it could be valuable to him. In fact, it might even be what he was searching for.

I can't risk losing it. I am not so godlike ... anymore.

He picked up the phone. "Prepare my bird, I'm going to England ... immediately."

•

11:45 AM
France

The call from Greer finally came.

"St. Germain, Solomon," Greer said, "Prominent addresses include three business and one residence in town. Outside of town, the next closest property is in Surrey—a country estate of thirteen acres."

Maelstrom stroked his chin.

When pressed, a human will invariably go to ground.

"Yes, I know the St. Germains," he said. "It will be good to see them again. Give me the Surrey address. I will pick you up near there. I am already on my way."

•

Noon
Surrey

Mady's heart raced when she saw the massive front gates of Chateau la Roche.

Here we will learn the truth about humanity's alien legacy.

The gates swung open by silent command and the Rolls-Royce drove through. She swiveled her head to watch the gates close behind them. Flanking the property as far as she could see were brick walls seven feet high. In the distance, she saw broken glass glittering along the top of the brick. Cameras sat at the gate, silent sentries.

Was it enough? She sat back in her seat, stones of trepidation crowding her heart. They drove through wild woods, coming out into landscaped grounds as they made the final turn. Before them was a great mansion of cream-colored marble.

"Oh, my," she said to St. Germain. "I guess I was expecting something a little smaller."

He smiled back with pride. "The original residence of wood and stone was built in the late sixteenth century," he said. "In 1755, the great Lisbon earthquake reached even here, splitting open the foundation and destroying that structure. This mansion was then erected over a massive subterranean vault. The huge rotunda with flanking wings is a classic eighteenth-century design."

Mady listened to St. Germain with half an ear, suddenly weary with fatigue. It pulled at her mind and her body.

What will happen when our pursuers arrive?

She shrugged her worries away as best she could and concentrated on the moment. She realized she was hungry as her stomach rumbled loud enough for all to hear.

"What did you say?" Carter chimed, his face puckered in concentration. He looked around the backseat of the limo, searching for the source of the noise.

She swung at him with the toe of her sneaker and barked his shin.

"Oww," he cried, eyeing her plaintively.

She smiled sweetly in return.

St. Germain laughed at their antics. "You have been through a difficult night, my friends. If you can go a little longer, we may find a way out of this." He turned to Mady and gave her a pointed look. "Translate the symbols, Madelyn, and I promise to feed you well."

The Rolls pulled behind the mansion and parked in a great carriage house. Henri led them through a small side entrance into the southern wing, moving with the same quickness and stealth he had shown all night. His actions reminded Mady they were still on the run.

They entered an enormous drawing room. On the walls were life-size paintings from several eras. One end of the room held a massive, Renaissance-style marble chimneypiece carved in gleaming marble. The high ceiling was arched, with barrel ribbing decorated to match the mantle and chimney. Mady was torn between the pressing need to hurry and the spectacle surrounding her.

"Will you be comfortable here?" St. Germain asked.

Mady eyed the solid mahogany secretary desk where Solomon had seated her. Nineteenth century, with lion detail in the front legs, she read the gold initials, *JFC* and the date *1816*. "Is this?" she asked in a hushed whisper.

"Yes," Solomon answered. "This is Champollion's desk—where he worked on the Rosetta stone languages. I thought it was appropriate for your work. Henri is bringing sandwiches. Will you make it?"

She sat reverently at the desk, pulling the chair close. "My laptop won't scratch this, will it?" she said, smoothing her palm over the glossy wood surface.

"Your laptop can burn the house down if it will translate the symbols," he answered. He gave her a curt bow and walked off hurriedly.

Mady worked quickly, satisfying herself with an occasional glance around the room. Soon Henri appeared with hot coffee and sandwiches of sweet pink ham and English cheddar. He left the plate for her on Champollion's desk with a casual salute before disappearing. Mady saw Carter and St. Germain eating at the far end of the room.

"Done," she said, finishing her program adjustments and her sandwich at the same time. She grabbed her work satchel and went to join Carter and St. Germain.

St. Germain took them through a large circular doorway. Mady caught sight of a magnificent eighteenth century painting of Egyptian deities in vibrant detail and she stopped to admire the ferocious leonine god depicted.

"Come, *cherie*," St. Germain called. "You may inspect it to your heart's content ... later."

She looked up from the painting and saw a steel security door recessed into the wall. It was utterly impenetrable and she sighed with relief.

No one could get past that.

St. Germain entered a sequence into a side panel and the great door slid open. They stepped through. The door sealed shut with a pneumatic hiss. "I believe we will be safe down here," St. Germain said as he turned to take the stairs. "Any tampering with the code or the door and the system will automatically lock down and notify the authorities. Come, I have everything ready for you."

The passage descended deep into the bedrock. Rough carved walls wrapped around smooth rock stairs that went steadily down. Mady looked at the ceiling of the stairwell and saw a conduit carrying in the electric. Circulating air fanned her face.

They descended twenty-five steps.

At the foot of the stairs was an arched doorway opening into an L-shaped cavern, with the short leg of the room extending into the darkness behind the stairway.

Mady stopped at the foot of the stairs. Carter stood beside her.

"Carter—" she said, reaching for his hand.

"I'm here. I know, I can barely breathe, my heart's pounding so hard," he said. She glanced at him and he winked, adding, "And I do believe there's a wobble in my knees, too."

She squeezed the comforting warmth of his hand and worked to calm her own racing heart. "This is it," she said. "All the sleepless nights, all the tears, all the questions—everything comes down to this room and what we discover here. I've already learned things tonight I wished I hadn't," she whispered. She tightened her grip on his hand and shook her head. "I don't know—"

He rubbed her chilled fingers. When she shivered in reaction, he stopped and held her before him. "You have a destiny here. Don't ever doubt it."

She looked into his eyes and marveled at the confidence shining there. She dared to smile. Again, she couldn't bear to let him down.

Together they turned to face the bare room.

On their left was a large walk-in vault set in the rock wall, its door of steel bars stood open. Against the wall opposite them was an old Tuscan-style kitchen table looking absurdly out of place in the chiseled rock room. She started to laugh at the incongruity of its presence—but then she saw the box in the spotlight.

Dark, yet sentient, the box sat, waiting for their arrival. Shivers shot up and down her spine. Here was even more proof of an extraterrestrial civilization on earth. The thrill of seeing the box sent a hot rush of adrenaline coursing through her body. Today, she thought, is the beginning of a new world.

What will we find inside?

She glanced at St. Germain. He stood off to the side, trying to be unobtrusive and failed. He watched, both hands thrust anxiously in his pockets.

Mady approached the huge Tuscan table with Carter close behind. Unwilling to take her eyes off the box, she set her satchel down on the table. Out came her laptop, all the while her mind twirling like a dervish. Carter stood next to her. Side by side, they gazed at the artifact from King Solomon.

The alien artifact waits for us, Mady thought. Seeming ready to tell the tale for which so many had died. Mady was immobilized with her fatigue and wonder. Carter pushed a chair against her knees, forcing her to sit. He pulled up another chair and sat with her.

Behind them, St. Germain paced, flickering in and out of the light in Mady's peripheral vision.

Blind to all but the black alien box, she took her bearings. Beneath her, the hard wooden surface of the chair bit into her thighs. Around her face a light air current gently fanned her hair and she was remotely grateful. Inside, her heartbeat was slow and steady, her breath oddly at ease.

"You are my destiny," she said. "Tell me your secrets."

The box was rectangular. She guessed it to be about fifteen inches high and wide, and about twenty inches long. The entire surface was a smooth, seamless, shiny black material she didn't recognize. She saw no place to insert a key. She arched her eyebrows in silent question at St. Germain who watched from across the room.

"Now you know why the box has never been opened," he said, walking toward her. "I assure you, there are no key apertures on any surface."

He reached into his pocket and removed a piece of cut crystal shaped like a four-sided pyramid, about one inch high. He placed it on the table in front of her. "We think this is a key."

"All this writing—" Mady said. Her mind was alive with anticipation as she picked up the crystal and rolled it in her palm. "After years of looking at just an alphabet, this is a library."

She squinted at the black box, pointing to precise locations. "There are symbols imbedded in the surface, copious amounts everywhere, some in short bursts." She paused, feeling the excitement sweep over her. "And in some places there is lengthy text." She shrugged with delight. "I have no idea where to begin."

Beside her, the two men appeared perched on her every word, their faces filled with obvious expectation. Before her, the laptop waited, poised and ready.

Time is running out.

Instinctively, she reached to touch the box. A quick look to St. Germain brought his permission with a nod. Her right hand smoothed over the alien box, surprised at the warm feel. She closed her eyes and let her fingertips skim ever so lightly over the surface, her senses at a peak.

With the key in her other hand, she thought about the lock that must accommodate that piece. She kept skimming her fingertips over the surface, searching, asking ... until she found a faint pinhole indentation on top, in the center.

She pulled a magnifying glass and a small flashlight from her satchel. Handing the light to Carter, she said, "There, hold it still." When he had the light where she wanted, she inspected the symbols around the hole. Carefully she entered them into her laptop.

St. Germain came to stand next to her. His dark eyes were fixed in total concentration on the laptop screen as she entered the symbols. Incredulous, he read the translation as it appeared. "Place here think open." He pulled back, uttering, "Nooo ... "

Mady couldn't help but grin. "While we were upstairs, I made my program adjustments based on what I learned from your Rosetta coin," she said. "The alien language, so far, is surprisingly similar in structure to English."

He reached for the key in her hand, clearly intending to open the box.

She closed her hand. "Let me read a little more before we proceed. You did say we were safe down here, so let me work with some of the writing. I won't be long."

Solomon stepped back and shoved his hands in his pockets, exhaling a long whistle between pursed lips. "No, you're right," he said. "I'm sorry, it's just been—"

Mady touched his arm. "I know, and your wait is nearly over, but let's take this one step at a time."

He backed away farther, giving her room.

She set the key on the table, her mind filled with the task and the box. "Can you turn up the lights?" she called out.

St. Germain hit a switch, giving her a flood of light. She ran her fingers over the surface, wondering where to begin.

"Where do you want me?" she whispered. She kept passing the fingers of both hands across the blackness until she found more impressions. Scrollwork so finely etched she couldn't see it with her naked eyes, and yet it reached out and caught her fingers. She grabbed the magnifying glass and examined the writing. She took her laptop and began entering the symbols.

Carter got up to join St. Germain. The two walked slowly, ears focused on the tapping of Mady's data entry. In silent accord they continued along the perimeter—expectant fathers in a bizarre maternity ward.

They followed the cavern wall back to where it angled sharply and slipped into darkness behind the stairs. Carter stepped into the shadows when St. Germain grabbed his arm to pull him back. "The earthquake I mentioned earlier—it left a crack in the bedrock. It runs back here—be careful," he said.

He turned on more lights, exposing a gaping fissure in the rock at Carter's feet. The crack was almost two meters in width and ran across the entire back section of the room.

Carter stepped forward and looked over the edge into the abyss. The light cast down for fifteen feet before the ragged wall face disappeared into darkness.

In a sudden rush of vertigo, he windmilled his arms madly as he seesawed out over the edge. St. Germain caught him by one flailing arm and snapped him back. Carter stepped away and turned about, calmly returning to his pacing. Over his shoulder he said, "Might think about filling that in, 'ol boy."

The two men continued their circuit, going from light to shadow, and back. Carter stopped St. Germain. Keeping his eyes on Mady, he asked, "Have you considered all your options?"

St. Germain's response was a brief huff of laughter. "Carter, bless you for being so civilized. Your cool head in the face of impending doom steadies me. What you are asking so delicately is, what am I going to do?"

St. Germain's laughter faded and he rubbed his temples. "How can one man be responsible for something of this magnitude? My family was vested with secreting the thing, not releasing or abandoning it." He stared at Mady, still bent over her laptop, and shook his head in despair. "This is not a decision I am qualified to make."

Carter placed a sympathetic hand on St. Germain's shoulder. "You have a tremendous responsibility, one I am glad does not rest with me." Seeing St. Germain's distressed face, he continued. "If this is any help, Mady believes a serendipitous chain of events, combined with exceptional planning on their part," he said, eyeing the heavens, "have brought the artifacts into the right hands—that being us, of course."

St. Germain's facial response was rifled with doubt. Carter grinned, coaxing. "Solomon, relax. The world has waited several millennia for this day. It can wait a few moments more. At the very least then, if you want, we can always do a vote."

Suddenly, the cave fell silent and they turned in unison to look. The screen on Mady's laptop flashed, *Translation Complete*. A length of text followed.

She stood, calling to them, her words echoing off the rock walls. "I'm going to read this," she said, "but you need to come over here and see for yourself."

She cleared her throat with a cough and began reading. "Be aware, there is so much more within, so much more without. We once struggled with greed, hatred and destruction just as you do. Thus we believe you must retain hope. By the grace of God we survived and ceased to destroy. Once beyond the destruction we achieved unparalleled growth and evolution. We became as gods ourselves with a love for all life. A desire to create. With this our goal we came to this planet because of the abundant life. We gave what we could because you are children. Our hope is you will evolve as we did. To take your rightful place as gods of creation, ceasing to destroy is the key. This will be your ultimate test. We pray for your intelligence and your survival. As it is with all children we can only provide the tools. Whether you free yourselves to claim your legacy as gods—or not—remains your choice and your adventure. The knowledge of this power is our legacy to you. Use it wisely."

Mady quivered as the final words reverberated in the silence. The message was too thrilling for her to absorb. Whereas earlier she suggested restraint, now she surged with energy. Her tingling fingers twitched with excitement. She declared, "This is deliberate involvement in the evolution of the human species by an extraterrestrial life form. We have to go on. I say we open the box."

The men stared at her with astonishment. She waited.

Carter released his pent up breath in one great exhalation. He ran a hand through his hair, struggling to speak. "Years of speculation ... that's one thing. But what they are saying is ... is ..." He stopped, at a loss, staring around, before finishing. "This is stunning. I'm with you. Let's open it."

She turned to St. Germain. He remained silent, obviously conflicted for several seconds before answering. "By all means, Madelyn, if you are ready, then do so."

Mady picked up the small crystal pyramid. She held it upside down with the pointed end resting in the pinpoint hole. For three long breaths she worked to still her trembling hand and steady the crystal. On her fourth breath her hand relaxed and she focused her thoughts on, *Open.*

Seconds passed.

The crystal stuttered alive with a fine vibration and locked itself in place by an unknown force. Startled, Mady yelped and jerked her hand away, stepping back in a rush. "I'm okay," she said, rubbing her hand. "I'm not hurt, I just wasn't expecting—"

She kept her eyes on the suspended key as she took another step back, rubbing her fingers. When she bumped into Carter, he put an arm around her and gave a squeeze.

The three of them stared at the box with its key precariously suspended. The crystal maintained its position for several seconds when a small panel in the top slid open and the key tumbled inside. The panel slid back without a sound.

They stood frozen in place, staring at the box on the huge Tuscan table. One second passed, then ten, and thirty.

Just as Mady opened her mouth to speak, the box began to hum. The top split in the middle and the opening widened until only the four sides remained. They collapsed outward, revealing a pyramid within. The pyramid appeared to be made of the same dark material as the box, and like the key, it was a four-sided pyramid, but about twelve inches in height. Each of the four sides of the pyramid contained a slot—three slots were horizontal, one vertical.

St. Germain looked at Carter, who in turn looked at Mady. Mady looked back at Carter and shrugged. "Whatever I expected, this isn't it." She asked, St. Germain, "Well, now what?"

St. Germain nodded. "Please, continue."

She returned to the table and inspected the pyramid. Three slots one way, one slot the other way. Thinking of her success so far, she placed her right hand on the pyramid and closed her eyes, letting her fingertips glide over the surface, wanting instructions.

Her fingers caught more of the delicate etching around each of the horizontal slots. She squinted at the fine engraving and laughed.

"Carter, your coin. And you, St. Germain, give me yours."

She took the coins and bent close, following her fingers with the magnifying glass. Her lips moved in silent supplication as she placed her Sumerian coin in one of the openings. Next, she put St. Germain's Hebrew coin in the slot on the side opposite from hers. That left Carter's Egyptian coin to go in the final horizontal opening.

She stopped. "Whatever we might think," she said, looking from Carter to St. Germain, "we are still playing with fire. For all I know, we might get … to another dimension … or something … very Star Trek-ish."

Carter cringed and brought one hand to his mouth, clearly aghast at her words. St. Germain stood with a blank look, as though she had spoken Martian.

"Okay, then," she said. "So, you say we dare?"

St. Germain stirred from his stupor. "It's too late to

turn back," he said with a quick look around. "For all of us. We must go on."

He and Mady waited for Carter, giving him time to make his own decision. "I agree," Carter finally answered, nodding at St. Germain. "The decision was made for us long ago."

"Then, here we go," Mady echoed as she dropped Carter's coin into the final opening.

The first two coins were resting in place partially exposed. When she released the third coin, it slid into its opening and then whisked out of sight. For several seconds they stared with intense anticipation.

Nothing happened.

"Cripes," Mady hissed, her breath exploding from her in exasperation.

Too much has happened in the last eighteen hours to get this far—and now, nothing.

"I swear," she said to the pyramid as she stepped to the table, her fingers twitching. "I will—" She reached for it, and when her hands were inches away, the other two coins dropped inside in a flash, causing her to squeal and jump back again.

Carter grabbed her and pulled her next to him.

St. Germain gasped and clutched his throat, his bulging eyes fixed on the pyramid.

For several long seconds, the pyramid hummed with a high pitch. Then a broad beam of light shot out of the vertical opening and hung suspended in a transparent, three dimensional hologram.

CHAPTER TEN

1:00 PM *Saturday*
Surrey

Three kilometers from the St. Germain estate, Jack Greer waited in an empty field, a nasty scowl plastered on his face and his mind rife with morose thoughts.

Everything is out of control.

His guts churned and apprehension tumbled down his spine. This assignment had created its own path, going over and around him, propelling him, in spite of his best efforts.

Memory of them, the girl's mother and father up in New York, seethed in his agitated mind. He could have stopped it then, could have stopped that crazy Mason—but he didn't. And now hell was here to collect payment for that day.

He wanted to stop it now, but despite his best efforts, this situation was out of his hands. There was nothing he could do to fix any of it. He couldn't change the past any more than he could change what was about to happen. Like a man cursed, all of his worst nightmares were converging to assure his life was a complete living hell—and yet, it was the dream that continued to drive him.

"You're just insane," he accused himself.

"No—" he spit back under his breath. "The dream is trying to tell me something, something I need to know before—"

The first *whop whop whop* of the approaching helicopter warned Greer of Maelstrom's imminent arrival. "What's so important?" he demanded. "What are you trying to tell me?"

Suddenly, the big Bell 430 rose over the crest of a wooded hill and hung suspended, its rotors spinning like the flitting wings of a hummingbird. Greer looked up. The One stared at him from the pilot's seat.

Greer hunched his shoulders.

No time, no time—no time left to figure it out.

The helicopter came in to land and Greer ducked his head. Dirt swirled around him on the winds of hell, bombarding his face and eyes, blasting his lips with grit. Without warning, the dream filled his mind, only this time the corpses opened their mouths, laughing and spitting dirt. They raised their dead fingers, pointing at him. "Like one of us," they chanted.

And then the image was gone.

Greer shivered and wiped his mouth on his jacket sleeve.

Ask and ye shall receive.

He spit once more to clear the grit from his mouth. "No!" he denied in a hiss. "I am still alive."

Shifting from foot to foot, he watched the big bird settle with finesse. He stalled as long as possible, waiting until the rotor blades drifted gently. He approached slowly and took a deep breath before opening the door.

Maelstrom's impatience was a palpable wall of energy. "We have places to go and people to see, Mr. Greer," he said, drawing Greer's name out with a powerful rumble. "I'd like to get going, if you don't mind."

Greer braced himself, swallowing hard as a sick foreboding filled him—but he couldn't stop. He looked up into the ancient amber eyes, and said, "I advise you to abandon this mission."

The One sat with spine erect, a deep rumble still bubbling in the huge chest.

"Nothing," Greer continued vehemently, "has gone right with this assignment since it activated last night. As it is, we are operating at a loss and it is my paid recommendation," he ground out, "that we retreat long enough to re-evaluate our intelligence. I have a bad feeling about this—and I must protest you are acting with haste and in error."

He finished in a rush and sucked in a deep breath. His insides quivered with adrenaline and his words rang in his ears with false bravery. *No sleep*, he thought, *and a belly full of regret—there's a suicide cocktail.*

And the dream, cruelly driving me ... to what?

He dared to look up, but not into those awful eyes. No, instead he focused on The One's elegant and likely exorbitantly expensive purple silk tie.

Here I stand all sweaty with dirt in my mouth, and you're wearing a five-hundred-dollar tie.

He felt the grit wedge in his teeth and his animosity flared. "I said," he declared hotly, "you're making a mistake."

On fire with his passion, he raised his gaze to the face—and in that moment, understood he was a fool. His passion evaporated, leaving him with a liquid, screaming desire to run.

What have I done?

Their eyes locked. Greer's light eyes were snared by the power of amber, immobilizing him. Seconds passed and Greer saw The One's hackles rise, releasing the pheromones.

Which meant it was too late.

Greer shivered in the wash of pheromones. Mortal fear, screaming and intense, manifested in the base of his spine, bringing a stunned paralysis. Water bubbled ominously into his intestines, inciting cramps. Further south, his gonads withered painfully in a search for higher ground. He tried to fight the chemicals, but he had no body to command. Stunned, he faced the beast.

The One gave him a slanted eye of disgust. "Sssshhh," he whispered. "Don't fight ... you only make it worse." He shook his head, frowning. "Why would you contradict me, when you know very well what will happen?" He pointed to the empty passenger seat. "Get in," he commanded. "I gave you a light dose because I'm going to need you when we get there. You're going, whether you want to or not."

Greer felt the first wave of fear recede as The One waited. After what seemed an eternity, the effects of the pheromones fell away like a wet blanket. Gradual muscle control returned, limb by limb. Then a sudden wave of nausea swept through him and he exhaled heavily. Gagging, he bent over and dry heaved.

Ah, yes, London. He recalled the first time—

It was 1999. In the orientation for Maelstrom's surveillance operation, all upper level managers who would be reporting face to face with The One were treated to a shot of pheromones.

"To give you some idea," Maelstrom said, "what you are dealing with."

Greer grinned with weak relief. The nausea meant his body was throwing off the pheromones. The heaves passed as quick as they came, leaving him woozy and light-headed. He sagged against the helicopter door— and stared at the great leonine face of his boss.

Maelstrom's head was large with bushy eyebrows sitting on the edge of his sloping forehead. The exotic, inhuman eyes were deeply recessed, bored and brooding, yet deceptively sharp. At the base of his long, flat nose were ultra-sensitive nostrils, delicately flared. The side of his neck housed the lethal stiff hairs, now at rest, lying flat against the collar of his fine, Italian suit.

Greer recalled the boys in the lab doing a work-up on the composition of the pheromones. He wasn't much for chemistry, but he was clear on one point.

The very first exposure always gives the most severe reaction. However, resistance can build, but only after repeated exposure in a brief period of time.

He swallowed hard.

Perhaps now is not the moment for insurrection. He climbed into the helicopter and fastened his seatbelt without a word.

The One brought the helicopter swiftly off the ground. "Not quite as much fun as space travel," he said, "but it's the closest I get." He grinned with pride, one lip curling to reveal a fang. "We'll be there in a couple minutes." He gave Greer a hard look. "You should be able to walk by then."

Soon they came to the St. Germain coordinates and a huge marble palace. The One settled the bird behind the mansion on the concrete area where the drive met the carriage house.

While they waited for the rotor blades to slow, The One donned his hat and dark glasses. "I have read all the files. I have been watching the St. Germains for a long time. It is quite possible they possess something of extreme value to me."

He slid his shades down and pierced Greer with his cold, animal eyes. "I want whatever they have," he said.

Re-adjusting his glasses, he continued. "I do not feel any of the three to be a threat we can't take care of ourselves. Stay well behind me when I release my chemicals and you will not be affected. When I have what I want, you know what to do."

Greer squinted and nodded, feeling the nausea creep back.

Beside him, The One laughed and slapped him on the back with his big hand, knocking Greer forward into the helicopter dash. "Cheer up, little man. If you do well inside, I may let you live."

Greer pushed himself upright. A quick glance showed him the silent threat delivered with those last words. He turned away, determined not to rise to the bait. But Maelstrom's mention of death stirred the topic in Greer's mind.

Dying—now there's an art form.

Many had died in Greer's presence, a good percentage of that death delivered by his hands. In that time he had nearly encountered his own death on multiple occasions. His proximity to death had often been measured in the smallest increment ... like right now.

Yet he ceased to care about life as a younger man would, for his life was more frightening than death. Because of his long association with death, he understood the "when" of dying was usually a surprise, but the quality of "how" was often an individual's choice. As with anything in life, you either did it well—or not.

Dying was easy, but dying well took a little more effort.

•

Safe in the cavern, Mady watched the light show beaming from the pyramid. Within a blink, everything in her life fell into place.

This is the most important thing I will ever do.

Beside her, Carter and St. Germain moved in close. Carter gave her shoulder a squeeze of confirmation. She looked up at him and nodded. "At last, this is what the coins are all about."

With stunning clarity, the hologram produced a layered image. In the foreground, a standing model displayed human anatomy and physiology. It rotated, giving them a comprehensive three-sixty view. In the background, the infinite black of the cosmos sparkled with the diamond pinpoints of stars and galaxies.

Mady spotted the three stars of Orion's belt. A laser thin beam of light went from the belt across the Taurus constellation to the Pleiades, and beyond. She strained to see what was the point of termination. Before she could determine or consider what that meant, the other side of the projected image began to move with a scrolling length of text in the alien script.

She flexed her fingers and curled them into tight fists. As she cracked the knuckles of both hands, she watched the hologram stream. Fingers loose and ready, she poised them over the keyboard. She picked a spot in the text and began entering the symbols as they passed in front of her.

Carter and St. Germain circled the hologram, peering into it as they came to stand beside her. The human body display changed, sifting through the layers of muscle to the bones, then down to the nervous system.

Mady continued to enter the text at a furious pace, even as she stole glances at the changing anatomy. Beside her, Carter pulled out his duplicate coin and set it spinning across his knuckles. St. Germain remained a statue, his eyes riveted on the hologram.

The image continued to change until there was just a view of the human brain turning gently. Then the lobes of the brain fell away and all that remained was a small cone-shaped nugget, exposed from its hiding place deep in the brain.

Mady puckered a quick, "Oh," and mouthed, "Pineal gland?"

Footsteps shuffled down the stone stairs and she tensed. She looked up as Henri burst into the room announcing, "We've got company."

•

Maelstrom and Greer climbed out of the bird and fanned out in opposite directions.

Greer's wobbly legs gained strength as he moved around in the fresh air. He checked the garage first and found the Rolls-Royce he spotted after the Café Dolce fiasco. He turned back toward the house and saw The One striding right to a small side door. The great nose lifted to the air and sniffed. A toothy grin appeared, and he called to Greer, "This way." He motioned briefly before turning, and opened the door. He disappeared inside.

Greer ran to catch up. When he reached the door, he peeked inside at a room filled with paintings. Ahead of him, The One slowly moved to the center of the room. Greer lifted a foot to step across the threshold, but The One stopped him.

"Do not enter yet," he commanded, holding up one great hand.

Greer halted mid-step and eased his leg back across the threshold.

The One lifted a top lip in a sneer of grudging appreciation. "Here is one worthy of the hunt," he said. "This is a man of impeccable taste and resources."

He stood in the center of the room with his hand still raised in command. The strong fingers flexed and curled as he concentrated. With eyes closed, he craned his head in a full circle, exposing his nostrils to every corner of the room.

Greer remained outside, stiff with anxiety. While he waited, his mind ran through a disappointing range of possible scenarios, each one resulting in his demise. Shaking off his morbid thoughts, he peeked through the partially opened door, watching The One. That deep rumbling voice came out in a purr, making Greer shiver.

"Since coming to this planet," Maelstrom said, "I have known all these masters." He nodded in recognition of the magnificent artwork on the walls as he continued to look around the room. "Ramses, Plato—" He looked at Greer and went on with his eloquent bragging.

"Galileo, Newton, Michelangelo—so many, they are too numerous to recall—many of your race have been brilliant. What you see here, Mr. Greer, offers us a measure of one man's worth far beyond the simple monetary value of the pieces. Solomon St. Germain is a very worthy prey. And now," Maelstrom said with sublime anticipation, "we are all here together."

The One sniffed delicately at the air. "This room cannot help but sing a subtle song of betrayal. From a rich symphony of bright scent, I can determine a great deal."

He paused and gave Greer a look that was dark with unspoken meaning. Alarm skittered down Greer's spine. He had no choice but to keep his face still and return a flat expression, playing poker with the beast. Inside, his heart was going off like firecrackers.

Abruptly, The One turned away, continuing his tour of the room. He walked to a mahogany desk and reached out to caress the chair pulled back from the desk. "The woman is tired," he said, "but she has spirit. I look forward to our meeting."

Once, twice, three times he sniffed, walking through the room. He turned with each rapid inhalation, drawing the scents of his prey into his sensitive nostrils. "Their whereabouts," he said, "could not be more obvious if they had left a trail of crumbs."

He moved to the far end of the great room and a massive, circular arched doorway. He walked slowly, his head turning side to side, drawing in the scent until he stepped through the arch. As he disappeared from sight, one great paw trailed behind, a single finger beckoning Greer to follow.

Greer stalked through the elegant room refusing to note the beauty it offered. He caught up with Maelstrom in a small anteroom that terminated with a steel security door worthy of a bank. He secretly sagged with relief when he saw it. "We can't get past that without a technician and tools," he said. He looked sharply at The One.

The One appeared unconcerned and a small shiver

of dread slipped into Greer's spine. He watched, mystified. This was his first occasion to go into the field with his boss.

Maelstrom paused to inspect a painting. He turned to Greer and preened with momentary glee. Pointing to a lion figure in the painting, he said, "The Egyptians called me Maahes, the Lord of Slaughter."

Greer stared at the painting, trying to comprehend what it meant to live for so many millennia, to have so much power, to decide the fate of so many. Throughout his career he had often been the instrument for many kills, but he was only a delivery service for decisions made by others. The real power, he knew, rested not with the killers, but with those who made the killing decisions.

Is that what the dream is trying to tell me?

Greer's pasty grin felt like a clown's mouth as his jaws ground in frustration and regret. How could he have made so many bad decisions, been so blind—so stupid? He was always nothing more than a pawn.

And now I'm left with a garden of corpses.

But he wasn't ready to join the garden, not yet. He had a score to settle first, and from the looks of this security door, their prey would live to see another day.

Humans one, animal zero.

Covering his smile of relief, he turned to leave.

"Do not move," The One said. "We are not finished here."

Greer looked over his shoulder. Disbelief clogged his throat.

The One placed his large hands on each side of the security keypad. He hunched his back and lowered his face so that his great nostrils hovered as close as possible. He inhaled deeply, and the fingers of both hands flexed in rhythm with each inhalation. Meticulous, he inhaled the entire surface of the pad.

Greer didn't want to watch, but morbid curiosity held his eyes fixed. At last The One lifted his face from the keypad and turned to grin with satisfaction.

"Ham," Maelstrom said with toothy pride. He bared all his teeth in a hideous leer. "They ate ham."

With a sure touch he carefully selected the sequence of numbers on the keypad. With a confidence born in millennia, he said, "It is so easy to be a god."

•

St. Germain looked up with shock at Henri's words. "How many and where? Can you identify them?"

"They landed in a helicopter out back," Henri answered. "There are only two—mademoiselle's abductor, and one other I could not see. They are right behind me."

Mady glanced up. Henri chambered a round into a .45. "Without the code," he assured her and Carter, "they cannot enter."

Mady returned her attention to the hologram and hunkered down over her keyboard. Regardless of what Henri said, she knew their time was up. She would not get another chance.

Carter came to stand at her side. His presence urged her to continue. In his hand she saw his coin tumble with a flash of gold. Henri and St. Germain collected on her other side to stare at the image within the human brain.

Time to fulfill my destiny.

Suddenly, she shivered with an incomprehensible sense of doom. A garbled sound rose from her throat.

"Nooo," she struggled to say.

Terrible trouble, she thought. We're in terrible trouble. Her fingers slowed and came to a stop as her shoulders slumped in a boneless heap. Moaning, she dragged her eyes to the arched doorway, where shadows skittered about the lower steps.

We are caught.

Afraid of what came for them, she turned to Carter. His face rippled with agony and he gripped the edge of the table with his empty hand. For a brief moment their eyes locked and shouted both fear and anger. He turned to look toward the stairs, but she refused to look.

She turned to St. Germain.

"They are … here," he said with difficulty. "How—" He rolled his head and moaned. "No, please, not like this … not when we are so close. Three thousand years—" He struggled to finish, but gave up with a whimper, his chin dropping to his chest.

Mady's mouth watered in fear. She looked past St. Germain to Henri. He shuddered and rubbed the back of his neck.

His neck hairs are rioting.

She watched, amazed at Henri's determination to raise the gun. He struggled with each halting movement, then stopped and bent over, moaning. When he straightened up, Mady clung to her hope, but he faltered and came to a standstill. Like Carter, he lifted his eyes to the archway.

She choked. Her legs felt like rubber cement, yet fear rippled through her intestines, screaming for her to run. She refused to be beaten, even as she turned resolutely toward the stairs. She held her breath, and watched.

•

Greer hung back at the top of the rock stairwell.

I hate going down into holes. Without exception, they are bad news.

Below him, The One was releasing his pheromones. With this, their first exposure, the cave's occupants would be completely paralyzed.

Greer waited. He'd had enough of Maelstrom's chemicals for one day and was glad to stay back, not trusting the airflow in this stairwell. From this relative safe distance, he watched as the big predator passed into the lower shadows and disappeared.

Holding his breath, Greer counted slow seconds. For his first hesitant lungful, he pulled his jacket over his nose to act as a filter. When he felt no reaction from his intestines, he dropped the jacket from his face and eased down the steps. The eerie silence brought a shiver.

"I follow the beast into an abyss," he whispered. He looked at his hands and they shook so hard he paused.

Get a grip.

He took a breath and shook out his fingers, giving his hands an eye-watering wringing. All was silent down below and he knew now it was his turn. He steadied himself and squared his shoulders.

At the bottom of the stairs was an archway. He peeked around the corner to a frozen tableau. The One retreated into the shadows, leaving Greer to finish securing the room.

He swept the cavern, his eyes coming to rest on the girl.

Don't worry—I haven't forgotten my debt to you.

He stepped past her to the Frenchman from Café Dolce. He eased the man's gun from yielding fingers, and struck him in the temple, knocking him senseless. "Frenchie," he said with a satisfied nod, "that's for making me look like a fool at the Café."

Thank me later for not killing you. If I live.

"What's happening? Who are you?" St. Germain challenged weakly. He struggled to stand over the fallen man. "How are you here? What … do you want?" he mumbled, hunching his shoulders.

Greer slipped the Frenchman's gun into his rear waistband and stepped aside. Behind him came the slippered soft shuffle of The One as he stepped out of the shadows. Like coordinated assistants in a magic show, Maelstrom and Greer traded places. Greer moved into the darkness behind the steps.

The One moved toward the light, his deep, commanding voice filling the cavern as he answered St. Germain's questions. "How am I here? That's a long story you don't have time for," he said.

Greer watched, sickened by the power play. A bitter taste on his tongue made him gag as The One began a mesmerizing show.

"As for who I am, you may call me Sir, The One or Maelstrom if you wish. My associate in the shadows with the gun is Jack Greer." His alien voice was smooth, his speech cultured, his visage terrifying. His captive audience strained to see more of that which they morbidly feared.

With a dramatic sweep, the hat came off, revealing the astonishing face of his alien species. The expressions in Maelstrom's immobilized audience silently mimed shock and rocketing understanding.

"Now, about what I want," Maelstrom announced. "What I want, I always get—" He gave a graceful wave of his hand, adding smugly, "As you can see."

Greer cringed, witness to The One at play with his prey.

Maelstrom stepped out of the light, and then sprang back into it, as smooth as a practiced dancer relishing a call for more. "But the all-important question is, Solomon," he said with a flourish, "What do you have?"

Greer knew a predator's game when he saw one. While he wanted to look away, he couldn't. He had to stay sharp.

The One moved with powerful strides and obvious strength. He smiled over his shoulder at Greer and nodded at the stunned faces of his audience. Infinitely pleased, he bared his teeth, offering proudly for all to hear, "You should have seen the look on dear Leonardo's face."

He moved among the frozen figures like a late arriving guest slipping into a party at the Wax Museum. He stood shoulder to shoulder with Carter, avidly inspecting what Greer could see was a hologram.

The One, his back to Greer, perched a hip against the sturdy table, cool and elegant. He leaned close to Mady, gazing at the laptop. Suddenly she jolted, and Greer could see the whites of her eyes from where he crouched in the shadows. Amazing, she glared back at the beast with a vigor that made Greer smile. He remembered all she had done to him and his team.

Give him hell.

The One reached out to touch her and she shuddered, but she stood her ground. The beast coughed, his tone smugly amused. "Your backbone is admirable, little girl," he rumbled.

Maelstrom gave a quick glance at Carter and St.

Germain. He sneered with disdain. "Your women are spectacular," he said with accusation.

He bent down to speak directly into her face. "When I see such spirit, it saddens me to know my species and yours cannot mate successfully." He scooted off the table and walked around her.

"Foolish men," he reprimanded, sliding past Carter. "If you had left your world to the women, I would have never made it this far."

With a snarl he preened his approval at her. Then his eyes locked onto the hologram. "However, as interesting as she is, I am here for these artifacts." He leaned down and placed one hand on Mady's shoulder. "Don't stop on account of me," he purred. "Please continue."

He released a visceral, frightening sound that made Greer's guts clench even at a distance.

Mady was startled out of her trance. She returned her attention to the rolling text of the hologram with a robotic turn of her head before placing her fingers back on the computer. She resumed tapping on the keyboard.

The One bared his teeth, turning to eye Carter and St. Germain. Going first to Carter, he moved in, circling. He sniffed, always the predator, and growled low in his throat. "Well, Carter, are you playing finders-keepers with me now?" he purred. "What do you have that I want, besides the pretty lady?"

Carter went rigid with a lurch. One hand jammed into his pants pocket and Greer wondered if he secreted some weapon.

Good luck if you do, buddy.

Suddenly, Maelstrom turned from Carter. With an ear-shattering roar of displeasure, he leveled a penetrating gaze at Greer.

Greer froze, emotionally impaled by the message delivered in Maelstrom's searing look. A trickle of sweat rolled down his back, and he ground more enamel from his teeth.

What the hell was that about?

The One turned abruptly back to his prey as though nothing had happened. He played with Carter, lunging and snarling into his face until Carter recoiled in fear.

Maelstrom pretended to wait for Carter to answer his question. Finally his lips spread in a parody of a smile as he taunted Carter again. "What's the matter boy, cat got your tongue?"

Greer saw that Carter quaked and silently applauded him, knowing what it felt like.

Maelstrom eyed Carter and grinned. Again, he swooped in close enough to exhale hot breath into Carter's face. When he was a hair's breadth away, he offered, "Sorry about your parents, boy. They were a mistake. Oh well," he finished with a shrug.

He pulled back again in a sudden sidestep, watching. A solitary bead of sweat trickled down Carter's temple and ran to drip from his clenched jaw.

The One rumbled with satisfaction and moved on.

Next was St. Germain, who still stood over the unconscious Frenchman. Maelstrom circled him until they came face to face. Maelstrom, with arms crossed, towered over St. Germain in a casual, yet threatening stance.

"This meeting has been a long time coming, Solomon," Maelstrom purred. "You have succeeded admirably in keeping this from me. It seems my suspicions about your elders were correct."

He dropped his arms and moved closer, hands planted on his hips, mocking. "As I recall—" he said, one clawed finger poised on his chin for effect.

"Ah, yes, the woman, she was made of steel. She surprised us with the poison, so we didn't make the same mistake with the old man. I guess you noticed he was missing the ring."

St. Germain's eyes spit his desire to wreak havoc, even while his legs and arms remained leaden. Maelstrom lunged into his face and breathed throatily with emphasis, "Solomon, what do you have that I want?"

St. Germain's face contorted in some failed effort until a single tear rolled from the corner of each eye.

"Just as I thought," Maelstrom sneered, his mouth a grimace of disgust. He moved to Mady's side, watching her fingers move across the keyboard. He looked up at the hologram.

Abruptly the humming in the pyramid ceased and the hologram disappeared. As one, all stared at the pyramid just as the three coins rose in their slots.

Maelstrom eyed the shiny gold discs and smiled. "Ahhhh," he purred as one coin was neatly plucked free. He held it to the light, reading. "*Knowledge is the Power. You are the Temple.*" He walked around behind Mady and stared down over her head at the laptop screen. For several long seconds he paused, rubbing the coin in his fingers. He put the coin on the table and bent down, bringing his face cheek to cheek with Mady.

Greer watched with interest, knowing how much power The One emanated. He was amazed to see the woman turn and boldly face the great amber eyes with a challenge.

Greer grunted with respect.

She's got balls. If we live through this, I'd like to shake her hand.

The girl and the beast connected eye to eye. Maelstrom whispered into her face. Greer watched, astonished as she leaned closer to hear what the beast was saying. She frowned, her acute expression inflaming Greer's curiosity. But when her eyes fired with an intense light of comprehension, Greer rocked back on his heels.

He wanted to know—

"What happened?" he whispered. "What did The One say to her?"

Abruptly, Maelstrom stood up. He slid his big hand into Mady's hair palming her skull and lifted her from the chair. He dragged her toward the stairs. Motioning to Greer, he commanded, "Get the artifacts and the laptop, we're leaving."

"Wait!" Carter shouted in a muffled choke. He took a stiff lurching step toward them. "You ... you don't have all the coins." He pulled his hand from his pocket and Greer saw his sluggish fingers handle something gold.

Maelstrom stopped and turned toward Carter, dragging Mady like a forgotten toy. "Would you dare to trade me, Carter? Dare you think you possess anything of more value?" he challenged.

Greer followed the conversation with one ear while he dropped into a crouch. Several feet in front of him, the woman hung like a rag doll.

He cursed. Time was running out, but he wanted to know—

What did the beast say to ignite enlightened comprehension?

Greer stared at her, silently commanding her to look up at him. She spotted him in the shadows. Using his face, his hands and his eyes, he begged her without words, pleading, "What did he say to you?"

She cocked her head.

Greer mouthed the question again. "What did he say?" But he was out of time, for suddenly Carter was shouting. Greer stood up.

"You need this coin," Carter shouted, his voice growing stronger. "This is the one that starts the pyramid. Without it, you get zilch."

Maelstrom snarled from deep in his chest. "Boy, I have bought and sold countless individuals. I own entire families and governments." He stepped, still dragging Mady with him. "I have bought and betrayed Kings, Presidents, and nations. I have started wars and destroyed entire generations."

He released Mady and stepped over her, giving Carter his full focus. His voice rumbled progressively louder in the cavern, his threatening visage growing darker. "What makes you think you can keep anything from me?"

Carter's face contorted into a damn-you expression as he drew his arm back and launched the coin toward the far side of the cavern.

Greer prepared to lunge for it even though he knew he'd never make it. He saw The One shake his head, then move with effortless ease as he leaped, extending his hand out like a mitt, snatching the coin out of the air. He landed across the cave, crouching on the balls of his feet. When he turned to them, his face was twisted with menace.

Carter staggered to Mady's side. He shook her and ordered, "Fight, damn it. Mady ... fight."

St. Germain began to stir. He rolled his head, coughing and choking, straining to speak. "You ... have no right," he called out. "The artifacts are intended ... for us." His face red with effort, he said, "I want to know ... where I came from ... where I'm going."

Maelstrom glared at them from the dark shadows behind the stairs. He sniffed the damp, fetid air from the crevice before glancing at the coin. He snorted a blast of derision, answering St. Germain.

"Dust to dust is all you need to know, Solomon. Beyond that, all the decisions are mine, at least for now." He growled and pocketed the coin, then leaped back across the cavern, landing near Greer and the archway.

Greer was rigid and alert against the cavern wall. The One's words echoed and ricocheted through his mind, stirring the stuff of his insanity.

Dust to dust.

His vision of corpses flashed, coming to taunt him. They grinned and laughed and the bodies parted, ready now for him to see. His heart cringed, terrified, yet his eyes searched on, heedless of the consequences, until he saw what was in the back, ready for him to finally understand.

The face on the last corpse was his.

All the pieces tumbled into place, pitching his world at a nauseating tilt. His long-simmering well of guilt, fear and regret exploded with sickening clarity.

He hadn't moved since being ordered to collect the artifacts. The One skewed him with a predatory look. The air turned heavy as the copper tang of fear crawled across Greer's tongue. He gulped and closed his eyes.

Standing just out of reach, The One delivered a brittle ultimatum. "Bring the artifacts and the computer."

Greer opened his eyes.

It's now or never.

At this range, there was no question of missing. Staring straight into the animal eyes, he lifted the gun and fired point-blank.

Before the gun's recoil jerked, one great palm wrapped around Greer's throat.

Next came the pheromones.

Greer's knees went weak and his guts trembled—but not as bad as before. Still, he wobbled, helpless and crushed with rage, his opportunity wasted.

How did he know?

Maelstrom bent over him, grinning into his face. The amber eyes glittered with ancient animosity and Greer knew they had seen murder and betrayal played out a thousand times. The answer to Greer's unspoken question rumbled from deep in the beast's chest.

"Neuro chemicals," The One said. "They carry the bite of betrayal. I smelled your decision … a long time ago. As such, this decision will cost you dearly."

Greer closed his eyes and exhaled for control. With an unsteady lurch he jerked his arm up and fired two rapid shots.

Pffft, pffft, the silencer sang.

But The One was ready. He threw up an arm and blocked the gun, making the shots wild. One bullet grazed his neck and blood oozed from a minor flesh wound. But his expression turned hot with indignant loathing when he glanced down at the flecks of blood. The loathing exploded into deadly malice.

He screamed, his rage straining every eardrum in the enclosed space. His free hand grabbed the gun from Greer and tossed it blindly behind him into the crevice. He wrapped his other hand around Greer's neck and roared, shaking Greer like a loose-limbed doll.

Terror pulsed through Greer in white-hot gushes, wringing more adrenaline from deep in his organs. He stiffened both thumbs and jabbed them viciously into The One's face, reaching for the eyes. Maelstrom craned his head backward, pulling out of Greer's range and tightening his grip on Greer's throat.

Greer thrust his knee into The One's groin and grabbed his suite lapels. He dropped to the ground with his foot pressed into the beast's belly. As he hit the stone floor, Greer grunted when the Frenchman's gun dug into his lower back—then his momentum sent the big animal flying in an arc over him.

Above him, The One's face glared in anger as he sailed by. At last Greer's neck was free of the strangling hands. He gasped and grabbed his throat, rolling to his feet just as The One landed behind him on the edge of the crevice.

The amber eyes spit with a killing rage.

Greer lunged to the left and reached for the Frenchie's gun at his back. Before he could lift the weapon, The One was there and the big fist once again closed around his throat.

Slowly, The One backed Greer up to the chasm until Greer's toes danced on the edge. The crevice yawned at his feet and the damp smell of open earth filled his nostrils.

If he shot Maelstrom now, he'd be dragged into the abyss. If he didn't, he'd be strangled and thrown into the depths anyway.

Animal one, Greer zero.

He writhed in absolute panic, twisting right and left. Ultimate failure ballooned in his chest. He clawed with his empty hand at the iron fist wrapped around his throat. "No—" he screeched through his constricted larynx.

Please, let me fix—

Immediately, everything in his mind telescoped to a still point. The chaos of his life and death struggle froze as a simple solution flashed through his mind. Relief washed over him. He saw the plan was a good one—and his only chance.

Greer relaxed his body and his toes settled on the sharp edge of the chasm.

All motion flowed like cold syrup.

The grunting of their struggle and their labored breathing echoed off the cavern walls, disconnected and as remote as a movie soundtrack in the next room.

The One's face loomed large and fierce. His vertical pupils glittered with a palpable malevolence. Greer felt the big hands on his neck tighten for the kill.

Greer enjoyed a smile of sublime knowing, drawing upon a reserve of strength he never would have guessed he possessed.

With a grimace of effort he grabbed The One's purple tie and wrapped the expensive silk around his hand twice. At the same time he pressed his feet into the edge of the crevice and pushed, leaning out over the chasm, feeling the open air embrace his backside.

Maelstrom grunted in surprise.

Too late. The balance and the power had shifted.

They hung on the edge of the crevice with Maelstrom's might and weight just counterbalancing Greer's suspended form.

Maelstrom released Greer's throat and flung his

arms backward like a windmill in reverse, straining to gain the edge.

Greer countered, stiffening his legs and arching his back.

Again they swayed out into space, daring gravity with each breath.

Greer sang with the heady thrill of power, savoring this moment, knowing it was brief. *No more garden of corpses*, he thought. Slowly, for he didn't want to fall into the abyss yet—he wanted more from his moment. He raised the confiscated gun.

Maelstrom saw the weapon. Panicked comprehension instantly filled his eyes. He strained and grunted, but he couldn't re-take control.

Greer spoke clearly. "Dying well is my decision."

His hand kept a death grip on the purple silk while he brought the gun slowly to his own temple. He smiled, joy watering his eyes, as he pushed away from the edge and pulled the trigger.

CHAPTER ELEVEN

10 Days Later
St. Germain Townhouse
London

In the private lift riding up to St. Germain's townhouse, excitement and dread fought each other in Mady's heart. She had been completely on edge since St. Germain's call this morning requesting her and Carter's presence. Not certain of St. Germain's intentions for disclosure, she hoped the coming meeting was to discuss the future of the artifacts.

Will humanity, at last, learn the truth?

She wasn't sure, and that filled her with anxiety.

"Madelyn, you're fidgeting like a two-year-old," Carter said with a slanted look. The effect of his glare was softened by the not-quite-serious tone lacing his words.

"I can't help it," she answered. "What is the value of making the translation if it isn't released? I mean, what's the point? Sure, you and I, and Henri and St. Germain—I mean Solomon, know what the ancients have left for us, but what good is that for humanity when it remains a secret?

"Today should be the beginning of the end for our old, unaware way of life," she protested. "We should be discussing the commitment to full disclosure—"

"Mady, you're preaching to the choir, here. But before you get all upset, won't you give him a chance to speak? The artifacts, after all, belong to the St. Germain family," Carter argued.

"The artifacts belong to all humanity—"

The lift came to a smooth stop and the door opened, cutting off the end of Mady's statement. She pasted a smile on her face.

Henri was there to greet them, smiling broadly. "*Mes amis*, here you are. Please come in, it is so good to see you," he said.

They entered the stately apartment and received a warm hug from their friend. Mady winced at the stitches and ugly yellow coloring that still smeared across Henri's left temple and cheekbone.

"It looks worse than it is," he said. He brought one hand up self-consciously to his temple.

"It looks better than it was," Mady countered. "I wouldn't be ashamed of it. Rather, be proud we survived, and let us all remember how helpless we were down there. See your wound as a reminder how fortunate we are to be alive."

"Do we have good news?" Carter asked. "Mady here is about to bust."

Mady glared at Carter and gave him her best Clint Eastwood squint. He pursed his lips and sent her a silent kiss, deflating her annoyance.

Henri smiled at them and answered Carter's inquiry

as to good news. "I have been instructed not to let any cats ... er, shall I say you will have to wait for him to tell you. Come, he is in *le' petite librarie.*"

Mady and Carter followed Henri down a long hallway of plush cream-colored carpet. The walls were emerald green watered silk, and filled with priceless paintings, each one a masterpiece. Degas, Monet, Rembrandt, Matisse, Renoir. The collection was beyond monetary value, reminding Mady with whom they dealt.

Le' petite librarie was a spacious yet comfortable room with soft leather furniture. One entire wall was glass with an expansive view of the city—the opposite held a fireplace bursting with a display of summer flowers. All remaining wall space was filled with deep mahogany bookcases packed to capacity.

In the center of the room, chairs and a loveseat surrounded a large low table set against an oriental screen of green and gold dragons. Solomon St. Germain sat there waiting for them.

"Here you are, and looking splendid my friends," he called out. "How good to see you when you are not running for your lives. Do come in, and please forgive my gallows humor, but I find that my *joi de vivre* has been resurrected to obscene levels. Please, come and be seated."

Mady sat on the loveseat next to Carter. Henri reappeared with an elegant silver champagne service intricately engraved with gold in a *fleur-de-lis* pattern. Crystal flutes waited on the table before them. With expertise, he opened a bottle of Dom Perignon and filled the glasses, serving everyone. When all was ready, he took a seat opposite his cousin.

"First," St. Germain declared, "I wish to make a toast." He looked down, long enough for a quiet aura to fill the room. When he lifted his face, pride and admiration filled his eyes. He tilted his glass toward them.

"Because of you, a great weight has been lifted from my shoulders, for which I am eternally grateful. I consider myself fortunate beyond measure to call you my friends and family."

"*Salute*!" He raised his glass to them.

Mady sipped her champagne and peeked at Carter. She wanted to believe St. Germain would release the artifacts. She could barely sit still. She felt St. Germain's eyes on her.

"Come, Mady, what would you like to ask?" he asked.

Mady set her glass down and blurted out, "Come on, St. Germain, don't tease me! You know what I want to hear."

St. Germain answered, "Please, you must call me Solomon. Aren't we close enough for first names at this point?"

"Yes, of course," she said smiling. Yet she felt a frown forming as she finished. "As for what I want, well, I won't put words in your mouth—I'll wait to hear what you have to say."

"Thank you," he said, with a nod to her. "As you know, tonight we celebrate completion of the first one thousand pages. I have copies of all the latest translations ready for you."

Carter spoke up. "Mady has shared a lot of what she and Henri have translated."

"And there are volumes more to come, Nick, which is why I asked you here today," St. Germain said.

Carter gave Solomon the nod to continue.

"Volumes about who they are and how they are related to us. Why they consider themselves gods and what hopes they have for us. Their words speak so eloquently and indicate great passion and an extraordinary love for life. They are beautiful to listen to," he said. "I am sorry that I did not live in their time.

"However, what is most exciting is they present us with an avenue of hope. According to them, there is still a chance for us to 'grow up' as they call it, just as they did."

Mady watched St. Germain with mounting expectation, uncertain if her greatest desire was about to be realized. Carter chuckled and rubbed her back with his hand.

St. Germain continued. "The more we study the alien symbols, the more we realize their linguistic structure. As you said, Mady, their language is very similar to ours.

"Look at your champagne glasses—see the first symbol on the coin. It is not only a letter, it is a representation of all they believe and what they are telling us. The symbol represents them and us, and a great deal more. They call this the symbol for Divinity. This is what I am most excited about."

Mady paused to assimilate St. Germain's words, impatient.

Divinity? What about disclosure?

"Solomon—" she begged. "Please."

"All right, but there is much I wish to share with you tonight—so you will forgive me these occasional moments of drama," he said with a wave of his glass. "I have more to say about Divinity later, but now, I would tell you about hope—something I have been without for a long time. Thankfully, that is history."

He shrugged in dismissal and set his glass down. Leaning toward them, he drew them in. "This material we have translated is complex, and the ideas are scientifically explosive. The deeper we delve into their message, the more potential I see—and that is what fills me with such monumental hope."

St. Germain's dramatic intro was delivered with such a mysterious tone, Mady shot a quick glance at Carter. He was absorbed in what was coming. She held her breath and leaned a little closer.

"The power," St. Germain said, "is seated in the pineal gland, as we all saw in the hologram. This tiny organ controls chemical production in the body." He paused for emphasis, adding, "And a great deal more. Because of its unique properties, the pineal works at several levels, and through more than one system. The nervous system and glandular secretions serve as its basic functions."

"Yes, we've learned all that," Mady complained.

He paused again and gave her the bear-with-me look while he poured more champagne, passing the empty bottle to Henri. St. Germain appreciated another sip, obviously savoring the drink and the moment. Seeing them waiting, he hurried on.

"Beyond the molecular level, this surprising little organ operates as a transducer, converting one form of energy into another. In this case, a release of neuro chemicals opens previously unknown pathways within the brain." He gave a flick of his eyebrows. "And that is where the excitement begins."

Mady fought the urge to raise her hand and interrupt. She clamped her lips tight and commanded her boisterous hand to be still. She had waited this long, she would last a little longer.

"This miracle occurs only within a specific frequency," St. Germain said. "It is generated by the emotion of compassion, and at peak levels of ultimate compassion, in combination with the sound of Divinity, the paths opened by the pineal gland enters areas of the brain we do not understand. What happens there is stunning and unprecedented."

Henri came and opened another bottle. St. Germain waited while the new bottle was passed around. "These chemicals—peptides—excite dormant receptors in the brain that in turn create an energy wave unlike anything known to man. This wave, then, is the bridge from thought to the quantum field and beyond into the physical realm."

He stared into the distance with eyes fixed and fever bright. He declared, with thick vocal chords, "This is literally the ability to command the atoms of elements; controlling matter with our mind."

Mady drank her champagne. She translated all this from the hologram days ago, and she had struggled to assimilate the enormity of it ever since. St. Germain's voice receded from her ears as a small hot spot of concern came to agitated life deep in her thoughts. She sipped her champagne and kept her face behind her glass while her heart pounded with unease, knowing St. Germain was making his case. Suddenly, she was afraid to know what this enormous bit of news meant to her goal of disclosure.

He wouldn't let this stop him ... he wouldn't—

She set her glass down, afraid her chilled hands would drop the fine crystal.

Carter said, "Mady and I have discussed these findings, and I still have trouble getting my head around this. Ultimately, I have to say this is beyond even my wildest dreams. The power to command the atoms could be scary in the wrong hands. Are we sure man is ready for this?"

"The emotion source for the power is compassion. Feelings in the lower ranges such as aggression, anger, and hatred, are unable to generate a frequency complex enough to fire the process. Only the divine emotions of love and compassion can produce the right frequency."

Carter shook his head with sadness. "All these millennia, we have waged war and destruction on this planet, denying ourselves the secret of real power."

Mady stretched her chilled fingers. Externally, she maintained a calm expression; inside she prepared herself for what she feared was coming.

Beside her, Carter sighed, the sound a mix of quick relief and exasperation. "Power commanded thusly must surely be one of the qualifications for 'flying with the gods again.' A power that is limited by one's intentions—perhaps that is the true definition of a god. I see why they call themselves gods."

While they conversed Mady remained disconnected, trepidation driving her heart. In spite of her attempt to wait, she couldn't stand not knowing any longer. She quietly asked, "So, what are you going to do with the alien artifacts?"

Conversation stopped. The look from St. Germain told her everything before he opened his mouth.

"I know you want to see the artifacts released," he began. "But I have decided that now is not a good time."

"You can't be serious," she cried. She jumped to her

feet, her fists clenched at her side, all pretense of calm evaporated. She cried out, suddenly panicked. "You have an obligation—"

"Yes—I have an obligation to the artifacts and to the legacy. Please, sit down and hear me out. Give me a chance to explain. I promise you, there is plenty of room for hope," he pleaded.

Mady looked at Carter, her heart breaking. Her eyes filled with water and she fought to keep the gathering deluge from running down her cheeks.

Carter patted her vacant seat. "Let him explain, darling. At least hear him out."

With a flop filled with agitation, she sat and dashed her hand across her eyes. Incomprehension clotted her throat, threatening more tears. Carter pulled out one of his linen handkerchiefs and handed it to her.

No disclosure.

She dared to glare at St. Germain, but her eyes rewatered, spoiling the effect.

"I want to see the artifacts released as much as you do," St. Germain coaxed. "Believe me. But just as important, Madelyn, I want them received."

Mady knew where he was going and the futility of his argument made her want to scream. "Humanity," she said vehemently, "will never be free from this cycle of aggression unless you shock them out of it. The idiots running this world have been screwing things up for thousands of years. They deserve to have their political and religious heads handed to them."

She stood again. She wanted to pace, to whirl and yell, but she was trapped between Carter and the screen of dragons.

"Cripes," she muttered and sat again. She turned on

St. Germain, unwilling to give up. "If there is a safeguard that keeps the power from being militarized, then what are you afraid of?"

Whatever his answer, the point was obviously beyond debate. She stood again, too upset to sit still, too upset to consider his rationale. Her hands fretted, twisting Carter's cloth for all it was worth. She shook her head as if faced with the end of the world.

"I can't believe you're not going to release this," she proclaimed. She threw St. Germain an unforgiving look before sitting down and closing her eyes.

"Please, *cherie*, don't angst yourself so," St. Germain chided softly. "As I said, there is room for hope, and a method to my madness."

Mady opened her eyes and rubbed her face, struggling to recover her faith after this disappointment. Reaching for the champagne bottle, she filled her glass and set the bottle back in the ice bucket with a thunk. She took several sips before sitting back in her seat. "Go ahead," she said with an angry wave of her glass. "Convince me."

St. Germain cleared his throat, drawing her reluctant attention, beating at her with his baton of hope.

"First," he began, "we will fund research based on the scientific principals and protocols outlined in the message. My goal is to have multiple research labs around the world establish identical results."

Mady glanced up sharply.

"I am assured this event will not take long," he said, giving her a look of absolute confidence. "Unlimited funding has that effect."

Mady shifted in her seat. Her foot came to life, twitching excitedly.

Unlimited funding.

That, she thought, *is a conspicuous motivator.* She nodded for him to continue.

St. Germain's tone turned serious. "You know, there are many that would kill us for possession of this secret. Maelstrom was not the only, or for that matter the worst, who would want to keep this information from the world. I personally can think of another, even more serious threat."

"If you go public enough—" Mady said.

"And see this story get laughed off the news because of the word extraterrestrial?" St. Germain countered. "Or have the artifacts confiscated by some military-industrial entity for exploitation."

Mady' foot stopped cold. She saw it just as he said.

We would be discredited and the artifacts taken from us.

"So tell me about this hope," she asked.

St. Germain sat forward, whispering. "The reaction sure to come from the power structures truly frightens me. If they get wind of this, they will no doubt want sole control. If that happens, we could all end up dead in the battle between government and religion over this all-important, but missing key from our history."

He picked up his glass and his eyes twinkled with conspiracy. "When we proclaim our research results in an international press conference, the world will sit up and listen. We'll hit them all at once, as you desire. I just want to be certain that there is no chance of the artifacts being taken or refuted in any way. I promise you, I intend to see this long lost part of our origins delivered."

"There will be a new world," she said, warming to his plan. Mady felt her excitement returning. "The paradigm shift will come ... and so much more. Truly, life as we know it will cease—in exchange for something infinitely better, for us and the planet."

St. Germain's eyes made the promise. "Our greatest responsibility is to make sure full disclosure happens and continues through to the apotheosis of humanity. Now do you see?"

Mady sat back, imagining events unfolding according to his plan and knew he was right—this opportunity must not be squandered due to haste.

Beside her, Carter sat quiet, spinning his champagne glass. Everything was prey to his hands since his fingers suffered the loss of his fake coin.

"How do you feel about this?" she asked Carter.

"I have to agree with Solomon about premature disclosure. Without irrefutable evidence, we'd be fools to speak up. I like his plan," he said.

He turned toward her and took one of her hands. "I know you want disclosure, but what you're really seeking is the changes that will come because of disclosure. With Solomon's plan, the new paradigm, along with mankind's apotheosis as Solomon calls it, has a chance.

"And until the time is right, he has the resources to keep everything safe. As you once told me, the ancients and the powers that be have put the artifacts in the right hands."

Carter reached for the champagne bottle. "Perhaps Solomon is right to have hope. Look at Greer, a man of obvious extremes. If he can make the ultimate decision of self-sacrifice, then perhaps humanity has more of a chance than we think."

"He wanted to know," Mady said softly. She gave Carter her glass. As he poured, she remembered Greer's face pleading with her. "He wanted to know what Maelstrom said to me. It seemed to be important to him. I never got the chance to tell him."

Carter asked softly, "What was that all about? You haven't spoken at all of your interlude with Maelstrom."

Mady hadn't mentioned the exchange with Maelstrom because she was still deciding how she felt about it. She cleared her throat, remembering the fire in those amber eyes. "He exuded an overwhelming energy. I think the energy of his species is too much for human physiology. I can't imagine any human able to stand his presence for very long, at least not that close. He was like a motor revved on high. He was just so ... intense."

A shudder stopped her.

"It took everything I had to stare back at him. My insides were shrieking, shrieking at me to run." She paused, her heart fluttering in her throat.

"His eyes were so beautiful, so mesmerizing, so frightening. Just looking into them was thrilling—because they were so inhuman."

Her body joined in the moment of memory. She sat rigid in her seat. "But the color—his irises were amber, gold and yellow, all lit with sparks in a field of glittering brown flecks."

Her voice dropped to a whisper.

"He spoke so low I had to lean into him to hear—and remember, at that moment all I really wanted to do was run. But his voice ... captured me and I ... I needed to hear what he had to say."

Every eye was on her, waiting for her to speak. She paused to swallow, to be sure she was clear, to make sure they heard. "He said, 'Time, infinite it may be, yet there is never enough.' "

Mady looked over her shoulder to Carter. "He frowned, and I could see there was something else he wanted to say. His brows came together in a heart-breaking expression of pain. The sparks in his beautiful eyes dimmed ... and his face showed a sadness so incredibly intense, I think it would have killed a human."

She stared into the past. "I believe he had more heart than the man I killed in the hotel. Since I was so certain that he, Maelstrom, was a heartless entity, his ability to express this level of sadness, to have felt such grief was ... both shocking and shattering. From the depth of my hatred, he evoked instead a tremendous sympathy—an emotion I didn't expect and could not have predicted."

Her fingers held onto Carter's ravaged handkerchief. Her voice came out a hushed tone. "At that moment, I felt his pain, and that rocked me."

She fussed with the handkerchief, straightening out the crushed and mangled cloth. "I have to believe that for us to know and communicate such pain, then perhaps the difference between his kind and ours is not so great. Perhaps he was not a monster, after all."

Pulling from her reverie, she asked St. Germain, "I wonder how long he was here. If his species has been around from antiquity as he claimed, it would explain a lot." The archaeologist in her mourned for what was irretrievably lost. "I guess we'll never know."

St. Germain shot a look at Henri, who cleared his throat.

"I saw that," Mady said. "Solomon, what do you know?"

"Actually," St Germain answered, "I have discovered quite a bit about Maelstrom. I was just debating whether to tell you."

The blood rushed with excitement in Mady's ears. Beneath the table her foot came to life. She tried to stay calm, but her inner child was jumping up and down. "I'd be interested in hearing if you know anything about him," she asked with deceptive calm.

St. Germain rose and went to a Louis XIV secretary, retrieved a stack of papers from within and returned, handing each of them a copy.

Mady peeked at Carter's copy to see if it matched hers. She scanned though the entries, reading at random. "Plato, Hippocrates, Pope Constantine ... Solomon, what is this? It reads like the best and the worst of human history."

At her glance, Carter shrugged. "Don't look at me," he complained. "I'm always the last one to figure anything out."

"These are the results," St. Germain answered, "of a little personal research I conducted in the family archives about the creature Maelstrom. I started out of curiosity, and finished amazed. I thought to share this with you so that you might understand what we faced in the cavern."

He signaled Henri before sipping from his glass. "I searched using key words such as The One, Maelstrom, lion men, and leonine god.

"While there were numerous references for lion men and leonine gods, I also found considerable responses for Maelstrom. The first records of him appeared in Egypt during the Twelfth Dynasty. From there, he was everywhere you see on the list."

Mady scanned her pages. Slowly her eyebrows inched higher and higher. "He was here ... all through our development? So what he said about dear Leonardo—" She did the math and whistled. "This means Maelstrom had to be several thousand years old. And yet he felt he didn't have enough time—"

"Yes, for better or for worse," St. Germain said. "He was involved with humanity extensively, and not just as a spectator. I believe his remark to Carter about kings and presidents was not idle bragging. For the last one thousand years, Maelstrom was primarily involved in Europe. He had deep ties to Brussels."

St. Germain shrugged and added, "References to the lion men dwindled to just Maelstrom in the last five hundred years."

He tossed the pages across the table.

Mady picked up a random sheet. She read aloud, astounded, "Pythagoras ... Alexander the Great—" She scanned down the list to the most recent names and hummed in wonder. "Hmmm, Winston Churchill."

She set the list down and retreated into memory once again. Finally, she asked softly. "Are they still there?"

"No," St. Germain answered. "The bodies have been removed from the cavern below Chateau La Roche. Mr. Greer has earned his right to eternal peace. He is laid to rest on the property in Surrey in a quiet corner of the garden."

He paused and stared for a moment at the scattered pages on the table. "Maelstrom's remains are being stored at one of my companies in Switzerland. I saved him for the genetic material. I think it may be useful when we have our press conference. He is further irrefutable evidence that we are not alone in the universe."

St. Germain turned toward Carter. "We looked for your fake coin, Nick, but it seems to have escaped."

Henri entered the room with more champagne causing Mady to glance at St. Germain. He was failing miserably at trying to hide another grand smile. "Solomon, you're holding back something else. Come on," she said, glancing at Henri with a grin.

St. Germain gave in, smiling ear to ear. "This is a momentous day with much to cover. Forgive me, again," he said, "—for saving the best for last.

"Since you left yesterday, *cherie*, Henri did a little extra work late last night. Remember in the cavern at La Roche, in the first message you translated there was a reference to us as children. At the time, I thought that reference indicated they tampered with our DNA. However, what we discovered just last night—"

Mady held her breath and leaned forward until the table cut into her knees. She looked at Carter. "Now what?" she mouthed. He laughed and grabbed her hand, just as mystified.

"They are the same as us," St. Germain continued. "Only older as an evolved race, much older and wiser. They recognized us in our primitive stage and considered us younger siblings.

"We were as children to them, so they showed us the wheel and how to count and write. They gave us agriculture and concepts of government and management. But they did not tamper with our DNA, because it was already ... perfect."

He paused, waiting for them. He lifted his hand to his throat where Mady saw the pulse trip rapidly. Excitement rolled off him in waves. He paused to catch each of them in the eye. "They say that the human form is ... common throughout the vastness of the universe, and that we did not begin on earth."

Mady eased back in her seat, her hand now raised to her throat, her pulse matching St. Germain's. She hadn't considered this. She was so excited about finding an extraterrestrial race that she hadn't stopped to think that humanity might be the extraterrestrial!

"There are more like us out there?" she asked. "Maelstrom was humanoid in form, but still a very different animal from Homo sapiens." She paused, her mind racing with this new information. She grinned and frowned in quick succession. "So, there are others like us?"

St. Germain shrugged, feigning nonchalance. "On this, all they have said is that the humanoid form is a favorite 'template,' as they put it. I believe they are preparing us to realize just how abundant life is throughout the cosmos."

Mady glanced at Carter. He held up his hands and shook his head. "Don't look at me," he mouthed.

She turned back to St. Germain. "There are others like us … only different, just as Maelstrom was." Suddenly she frowned and sat up, alarmed. "Solomon, do they say if this power we have is—"

"Ahh, and so you have it," St. Germain rushed to answer. "Of course, you would be quick to see the importance of the details. But this is the most important part of all, for it is the seat of our hope."

He scooted forward to the very edge of his chair and whispered, "The gift is special … and while there are other life forms with our basic shape, they do not have the gift. They say the power of Divinity is for Homo sapiens only."

Mady whistled and lifted her eyes heavenward. She chuckled.

Carter pulled back, looking at her. "What has you so

tickled?"

"Oh, I'm just laughing about humans as the ET—that has to be the joke of the millennia." She smiled and tucked his arm in hers, pulling him beside her. "It's all so fantastic. I can't help but wonder just how far we can go."

St. Germain wore his wicked grin again and Mady knew he had more to reveal. Henri sat relaxed, holding his champagne glass. When he saw her questioning gaze, he shrugged and smiled.

"Solomon?" she asked quietly.

St. Germain poured more champagne. "You are right, I have one more surprise," he said with a wink.

Mady sat up in her seat. Beside her, Carter chuckled and rubbed her back. "Solomon, please, tell us—she's going to explode," he said.

St. Germain leaned out, drawing them back again. Conspiracy invaded his voice as he asked, "Remember the coins and their messages? *Knowledge is the Power. You are the Temple.* Here, we understand that the knowledge they speak of is about activating the pineal gland."

He stopped to pour from the newest bottle, and Mady feared she couldn't keep up or she'd get the spins. After their glasses were filled, he continued.

"Now recall the Egyptian coin and its message, *Find Your Power in the Greatest Temple,* and consider the location where the coin was found—at the base of the Great pyramid. If we know the power is within our bodies, then what is the connection to a pyramid?"

The question hung, challenging them until he whispered, "The Great pyramid is an example of what can be done with the power in an activated pineal gland.

The ancients left the great pyramid as a reminder of our potential. Listen to this." He picked up a sheet of paper from the table, reading.

"Our pyramid looms greatly and larger than life as a reminder to you the children of gods. Let all see what you are what you can do. See and remember. See and know the pyramid shouts to you. Hear your internal response. I, too, can create. Hear the message and know such greatness lies within you. Stand tall with the knowledge of your potential. Know your goodness. Be all-powerful and be set free.

"See and remember," he finished, "Know and be mighty."

He set the paper down. "They built the most perfect geometric structure on earth using the power of the pineal gland and the frequency of the Divinity symbol."

Solomon's words made Mady's head spin with realization. Her thoughts took off, leaving her behind to stare blankly, trying to picture the Divinity process. The symbol, the sound, and the gland creating matter by eclipsing both time and space—material manifestation through non-material effort. She shifted in her seat with the vision of these ancients building the Great pyramid with their thoughts.

God gave me this gift.

Within her heart, a tiny glow of understanding awakened and she felt St. Germain's faith.

"Tell us more about the pineal gland power," Carter said.

"—the Divinity power," Mady added.

"This power—the Divinity power as you call it, is the new paradigm," St. Germain answered. "The ancients say awareness will begin slowly, but as more people on the planet are exposed to the protocols, the vibration will entrain with others to initiate and spur an emotional evolution.

"Sort of a one-hundred-monkey scenario, if you will. When the critical mass is reached—unbelievably a number as small as ten thousand people planet-wide—then the glands will begin to awaken *en masse* globally. My friends, we shall be a part of initiating this process, and witnessing the transformation of mankind."

He clasped his hands in a pose of exultant prayer. "We must reach this pinnacle that is our legacy, our destiny. That is why I am beginning research now so we can start this change, this transformation, our apotheosis."

Mady chewed her lip and wondered if mankind would have the strength to claim this legacy; they had been on a course of constant aggression and conquest since the first dawn. It was no wonder Maelstrom's race had been successful—he was just another predator in the pack against humanity. "What a shame the ancients expressed no intention of coming back," she said.

"I agree, a shame, as nothing so far indicates their return," St. Germain answered. "We apparently are meant to learn the rest on our own. It saddens me to think of never knowing them. They gave us so much.

"However," he rushed on, "I believe they felt the same way about us, knowing they would not be here when we 'grew up'. They had much to say on pyramids, and there is something more to interest you."

He passed around a new bottle of champagne and the sly tone of his voice made Mady sit up. She glanced at Carter and he pulled her closer.

"The ancients tell us we have a special journey ahead, concerning our destiny as a species. They are scarce with details, indicating only that someone will show us how to become—they call it entangled—whatever that means.

"But what's even more interesting," he said, his eyebrows lifting suggestively, "is the Great pyramid is far more ancient that we suspect."

Mady was too deep in overload to speculate what this might mean. She took a small sip and focused on the champagne bubbles dancing across her tongue while her mind ran with possibilities.

"The great pyramid was built," St. Germain continued, "for a variety of reasons. And the ancients say there are other pyramids 'in the neighborhood.'" He paused and pierced them each with a direct look that indicated even more mystery. Mady wondered what 'in the neighborhood' meant to the ancients.

Solomon answered her very thoughts. "From this, we must understand that the ancients go well beyond earth, and that earth is not the only planet nearby with such a pyramid."

Mady felt her spine wiggle with pure excitement. While archaeology was often tedious and boring, this rush of discovery was her addiction. She held her breath, anxious to hear St. Germain's words.

"As Mady said, we are the ET. Follow the eyes of your ancestors, we are told, and 'see what your ancestors revered. There is the place of your origins.' So far, that is the only clue they give."

Mady looked at Carter with a question in her eyes. *What does this mean?*

His eyes were a well of little boy mischief and promise. "Let's go see," he said softly.

"How do you do that," she asked, teasing him in return. She reached for him and tucked her hand into his.

"I was just going to ask you the same." He squeezed her hand.

She quivered with champagne and good will. Her earlier misgivings were long gone, now replaced with more ideas and excitement than she could handle. Her heart hammered with an overload of thrill, and she sipped her champagne, glad there seemed to be an endless supply.

St. Germain smiled at them, rubbing his hands together in anticipation. "We have a new task now, Mady and Nick. No longer are the St. Germains sole custodians of the secret. You two must join me as Gatekeepers to the new paradigm. With this Divinity power, the blueprint for a new civilization will come, just as the introduction of agriculture and writing brought a new world to our ancestors.

"I truly believe we have a chance to become as wise as they did—and my goal is to bring this transformation, our apotheosis, to the human race. I expect an awesome journey, my friends, and I hope I can count on you to be there with me."

Mady clapped her hands to her mouth with a gasped, "Oh!" She grabbed Carter's arm, shaking him. "Nicky."

Carter's glass was knocked askew, spilling the remnants of his champagne on his trousers. He snatched up his badly weathered cloth from the table and dabbed at his pants leg.

When the spill was contained, he set the cloth back on the table and reached for the bottle. His usually cool eyes danced with a new challenge. "I would like to make a toast," he said, passing the champagne around. When everyone was ready, he raised his glass.

He looked at St. Germain and Henri, before coming to rest his gaze on Mady. His eyes sparkled with adventure as he announced, "To us! To the artifacts that will transform humanity! To the journey ahead!"

Mady felt the old tingle of excitement return. Her lips slid into a smile that grew as she warmed to the full impact of the idea. "To our transformation," she said, lifting her glass. "To us!"

St. Germain and Henri chimed, "To us!"

Mady's heart and her head were spinning between the champagne and all the news. Now there was so much before them. *Where does humanity go from here?* she wondered.

"In order to claim this legacy," she said, "we must stop seeing what we perceive as our differences—differences in race or species—and realize instead how much we hold in common.

"If Maelstrom can have a heart," she proclaimed, "and Jack Greer can be a hero, then I believe you're both right—there is hope for humanity."

St. Germain sat up. His eyes were alive with conviction and the zeal of the prophet rang in his words. "Understanding the science of this discovery has renewed my faith in mankind," he said. "And renewed my faith in God's will … and His intent.

"For such power to be a gift from the Creator and not a freak of evolution is enlightening in itself. To call this the Divinity power is appropriate. When the ancients said we were made in God's image, who knew how accurate that statement would prove to be? I think of Jesus teaching the power of love and this now has new meaning for me. I believe he was preaching the science of compassion. He was telling us then how to claim our legacy.

"All this time," he continued, "We thought faith was about our faith in God. But the Divinity power is about God's faith in us, and our ability to claim our legacy. For Him to give us this gift, He must have had tremendous hope. How can I not feel elated," he asked, "when God has shown so much faith in us?"

He stopped to fill his glass. "I have faith, Mady, Nick—faith that humanity has a future ... a spectacular one filled with infinite possibilities."

He raised his glass to the heavens.

"To the Divinity power. Let it prove what so many would deny, that far more than we can imagine or even suspect is waiting for us. Both within ... and without."

•••

The ROAD to BABYLON

This electrifying sequel to the story you just read is coming to you in the spring of 2014!

Dana Lyons

Dana Lyons lives in the mountains of western North Carolina with her husband, Randy, four cats and two horses. She loves to travel and cook, try new wines, study quantum physics, and discover new mysteries of the heart and mind. Says Lyons, "If you believe enough, if you love enough, you can draw upon a power to create the life and love of your dreams. Love is a force that comes from within, yet steers the course of your life as if from the faraway stars."